水琴

The
Water Lyre

許其正　著作／英譯
Prose Poems & Translated by Hsu ChiCheng

水琴（代序）

有一條小河，從我小的時候流來，輕輕緩緩地，流成了一架水琴，一直在我的心靈深處。

河的兩岸有許多水草和岩石等。它們便是造物者創設的萬千琴弦。河水是彈琴的手指，尖細而修長，日夜不停地調撥著琴弦，靈活而熟練。

多像一名少女在彈琴！她把所有的深情凝聚在指尖，傾注到琴弦上，再由琴弦化為一隻隻彩蝶，裊裊飛昇，飛向她夢中的白馬王子。

那是小提琴？抑或是七弦琴？琵琶？胡琴？或者鋼琴？……

是一曲小夜曲？抑或是詠嘆調？抒情詩？宋詞？元曲？……

一曲接著一曲。那是造物者嘔心瀝血的創作曲。

琴音輕緩而柔和，悠長而纖細，深情款款，千迴百折，縈縈不絕，久久不散……。

它們是一朵朵星花，濺滿小河兩岸，閃爍著星星點點的光芒……。

它們輕揚起一片喜悅、和樂，驅去所有的不快、憂愁……。

潺潺、淙淙、琮琮、叮叮、噹噹……那是水琴在彈奏，輕輕緩緩地，柔柔和和地，從我小的時候開始，一直在我的心靈深處……。

The water lyre (In Lieu of Preface)

There is a river, flows from my childhood, slightly, slowly, flows into a water lyre, deep in my heart.

There are many water weeds and stones on the banks of the river. They are millions of string created by the Creator. The river water is the finger of the lyre, keen and long, plays the strings day and night ceaselessly, nimble and skilled.

How does it like a girl play the lyre! She holds her deep emotion with concentrated attention on her finger points, pours to the strings, turn into colourfull butterflies one by one, raising curl upwards, flies to her prince charming in her dream.

Is it the violin? The seven-stringed plucked instrument? The Pipa? The huqin? Or the piano?...

Is it the serenade? Or the aria? The lyric poetry? The Sang Ci? The Yuan Qu?...

One melody follows one melody. It's the created melody by the Creator strains his mind.

Slightly, slowly, and soft, long and exquisite, deep emotion in great earnest, kilo wind and hundred curl, linger and linger ceaselessly, don't disperse for long...

They are a flower and a flower, spatter fully on the river back, sparkle rays of light a bit and a bit...

They raise slightly roll of joyousness, gentle and pleasant, drive away whole the unhappy and worry...

Gurgling, murmuring, bubbling, ding-ding, dong-dong... it's the water lyre playing, slightly, slowly, soft and soft, comes from my childhood, within my deep heart still...

目次

早起的鳥兒

我在距我所住的鎮上約十公里的一所鄉間學校教書。那裡有許多不方便的，如買不到文具簿冊、家事材料等等。學生們大多在開學前買齊，或利用例假日乘車到鎮上買。有些和我比較親近的學生，便託我代買。我常常變成她們的義務採買。

學生託我代買東西，通常我總是在當天回家便買好，次日帶去，從不負她們所託。但是，有一次我卻忙忘了，受託那晚我沒去買，直到次日清晨要上班時才想起來。

那是一個學生要我幫她買三捲淺黃色的北京紙。鎮上有三、四家材料店，我原以為一上街很容易就可買到的，沒想到卻沒有買到。

我最先到我平日常去的那家，結果是關著門；再到鎮上最大的一家，也關著門；然後再到另一家，結果還是一樣：關著門。我正想是否硬給敲開門時，突然想起還有一家，乃抱著姑且一試的心裡前去，沒想到竟然在這我最不常去的一家買到了。全鎮就只有這一家材料店主人已起身，開了門做生意。

由於這緣故，我對這家材料店的印象丕變；我也決定，自此以後，都找這一家。

我在往學校的路上，一直在心中玩索著西洋這一句諺語：「早起的鳥兒有蟲吃。」

是呀！這句話，果然蘊有無盡的深意。

The early bird

I teach in a countryside school far from my town about ten kilometers. There are many inconveniences, for instance, can't buy writing materials and books, materials of housekeeping etc. The students almost buy all of them before school beginning, or take the bus to town to buy them on holiday. Someone who is on intimate terms with me often ask me to buy. I frequently am their duty buyer.

I often buy the things the same day when they asked me to buy, and bring for them in order not to break the promise. However, there is one time I forgot it, not buy it I promised that night, think it of till next morning I want to go to work.

They are three rolls of the yellow Peking paper which the students asked me to buy. Three or four shops are on the town, I think originally it's easy to buy them as I go to the street, but it unexpectedly I haven't bought them.

I went to the shop I often used to buy first, but its door is closed; I go to the biggest one again, it's closed also; then I go to another shop, the result is the same: door closed. I suddenly think of there is a shop still while I guess to knock the door hard and fast, I go there just to make a try, unexpectedly I bought them at that shop I scarcely buy. It's the only material shop in the town which opens the door to sell.

Due to this reason, my impression about this shop has a great change; I also decided from now on, I will go to this shop to buy.

On the way to school, I ponder a proverb of the West: "The early bird catches the worm."

Yes. It really contains profound meaning limitlessly.

晚霞花園

一抬眼，只見一座晚霞花園輕懸在西方天邊，燦爛輝煌，明麗閃亮，如幻似真……

園裡錯列著各種形狀的花圃，有圓形的，橢圓形的，半圓形的，正方形的，長方形的，菱形的，三角形的，還有不規則形的，雜然紛陳，一一羅列……

花有盛開的，有半開的，有微開的，有含苞未開的，花朵、花苞、花蕾，交相錯雜，襯以綠葉……

花色紛繁多彩，多種多樣，紅、黃、白、紫、藍、靛以及許多種顏色在同一朵花上的……

是玫瑰。是香蘭。是荷。是菊。是紫薇。是榴花。是向日葵。……

蜜蜂飛來了，蝴蝶飛來了，飛蛾也飛來了。牠們翩翩飛翔著，穿行在群花間，悠遊來去，怡然自得，採著蜜，傳播著花粉……。

當然，也有人穿行在花間。那個是園丁吧！看！他噴水澆花，又除著雜草呢！那些是賞花人吧！他們行走在花圃間的走道上，從一個花圃到另一個花圃，停停走走，走走停停，指指點點，時而彎下腰，伸手去牽扶起花兒來細瞧，來嗅聞，來品味……

這，不用說，是造物者手握夕陽這隻彩筆在雲上創作的畫了。祂揮灑著。祂繪畫著。祂付出了所有的心血，乃有了這一座晚霞花園輕懸在西方天邊，來愉悅我……

The Afterglow Garden

Raise my head, I just view there is an afterglow garden hangs slightly on western azure, brilliant and splendid, bright and radiate, as dream as illusory...

There jumbled the flower nursery of many shapes, that is, the round, the ellipse, the semicircle, the square, the rectangular, the rhomb, the triangle, and the irregular, appear miscellaneously, included within one by one...

The flowers are fully blossom, half blossom, slight open, be in bud, the flower, the bud, the flower bud, mix together, set off the green leaves...

Numerous and complicated the flower colour, multicoloured, there are red, yellow, white, purple, blue, indigo-blue and many kinds of colour on a flower...

May it be the rose . May it be the orchid. May it be the lotus. May it be the chrysanthemum. May it be the crape myrtle. May it be the sunflower...

The honey bee comes. The butterfly comes. The moth comes. They flutter, shuttle among the flowers, leisurely, fell happy and contented, gather nectar, disseminate pollen...

Of course, there is someone shuttle among them. May he's the gardener. Lo! He waters the flower, and also he weeds. And these are the men appreciate the flower. They walk on the path among the flower nurseries. From one flower nursery to another flower nursery, they now walk now stop, now stop now walk, point and dot, sometimes bow their waists and stretch their hands to hold the flowers to peer them carefully, to smell them, to appreciate them...

Wordlessly, this is the picture created by the Creator who grasps the coloured pen of the setting sun in his hands. He wields. He paints. He offered all his painstaking care, then there has this afterglow garden hangs slightly on western azure, to make me so jubilation...

啊，沉醉

　　吱吱地，蟬鳴著，在夏日，在鄉間，在果園，在林稍，一陣過了又一陣接上來……。

　　最先是一隻，然後其他的也響應了，一隻，二隻，三隻……終於，是百隻千隻，是千隻萬隻，鬧不清有多少隻在鳴唱了。

　　牠們盡心竭力地鳴唱著，看那樣子，真是施展出了渾身解數，要把夏日鳴唱得極為熱鬧。

　　東面有著蟬鳴。西面有著蟬鳴。南面有著蟬鳴。北面有著蟬鳴。……這許多蟬鳴果然來自何方？

　　有一片濃霧瀰漫在林稍。有一片顫搖和迷幻展翅在枝葉間。……

　　有一片喜悅在空間遊行。有一片清涼在空間散布。……

　　是一支支鼓吹，吹出長長的音調，久久不絕。彷彿可以清楚看見一個鼓吹手，在認真用力地吹著，在古典的廟會、宴會……。

　　是一隻隻可愛的小狗，伸出長長的舌頭，舐著人的肌膚，癢癢的，恬適的。

　　是一陣陣霏霏細雨，飄灑而下。啊，不，不是細雨，是一陣陣霏霏灑灑的小酒滴，令夏日沉醉，鄉間沉醉，果園沉醉，林稍沉醉，人們沉醉……。

　　啊，沉醉！在這世界上，任何沉醉都是美好的。

Oh, Be Intoxicated with

Creak, creak, the cicada chirp, in the summer, in the countryside, in the orchid, on the top of the tree, a spell takes the place of while a spell is over…

One is the first, and then the other respond to, one, two, three… at last, hundred and thousand, thousand and ten thousand, it can't make clear of how many are they chirp…

They chirp the best and put their heart and soul into the chirping, it seems that, they pour out as possible as they can, wish to chirp the summer into most bustling.

There are the cicadas chirping in the east. There are the cicadas chirping in the west. There are the cicadas chirping in the south. There are the cicadas chirping in the north… Where are those so many cicadas come from?

There is a scene of joyousness parades on the space. There is a cool and refreshing spreads on the space…

It must be the trumpet one and one, play the long and long tune, ceaselessly for a long time. It seems that there can see a trumpet, makes an effort to blows it, on the classic temple fair, on the dinner party…

It must be a lovely tiny dog, stretch his long and long tongue, to lick the skin of person, ticklish, calmly…

It must be a spell and a spell of drizzle, floating down, oh, no, not the drizzle, it's the tiny liquor sprinkling, let the summer be intoxicated with, the countryside be intoxicated with, the orchid be intoxicated with, on the top of the tree be intoxicated with, and people be intoxicated with…

Oh, be intoxicated with! All will be fine while there are intoxicated with on this world.

思維那隻小鳥

思維那隻小鳥，展翅飛翔著，搜尋著。

牠時而收縮著兩支翅膀，讓全身疾飛向前，倏忽而逝，如一支電射而過的箭矢；時而平展著兩支翅膀，緩慢悠然地滑翔著，如一艘在平靜的海面漂航的小船……。

牠飛向前，轉飛向後，飛向左，飛向右，飛向上，飛向下，飛向任何方向，並且飛向古往，飛向將來，在現實中飛翔，在幻想中飛翔。——這是一隻奇異的小鳥。牠飛進時間和空間的組合裡……

牠飛翔著，搜尋著，時而高飛，時而低翔……。

牠在忙什麼？

牠是在搜尋著牠的獵物。——一隻蚊子便是一隻雄獅。一隻飛蟻便是一隻大象。一隻小蟲便是一隻花鹿。所有的獵物，對牠都是一種喜悅。

牠是在搜尋牠的寶藏。——有許多美食、金銀、玉器在等待牠去尋獲。有許多哲理、文學、藝術甚至自然科學的精義在等待牠去擁有。

前面許是漆黑昏暗，許是光明燦爛，許是風雷雨雪，許是模糊朦朧，許是深奧幽玄，許是懸崖峭壁，牠都通行無阻，直入無礙……。

天空任鳥飛，啊，思維，你這隻小鳥呀，且儘量去飛翔，去搜尋吧！

That Tiny Bird of Thought

That tiny bird of thought, spreads his wing, soaring, searching.

He sometimes contracts his two wings and soars quickly, elapses instantaneous velocity, like an arrow electricity-like; sometimes spreads equally his two wings, soars slowly and leisurely, as a boat roams on the calm sea...

He soars forwards, soars backwards, soars leftwards, soars rightwards, soars upwards, soars downwards, soars to every direction, and soars to the ancient times, sours to future, soars within the reality, soars in the fantasy. - He's a queer tiny bird. He soars into the combination of space and time...

He sours, searches, now high now low...

What does he busy?

He searches his prey. - A mosquito is a lion. An ant is an elephant. A tiny insect is a chital. As to him, all the prey is his joyousness.

He is searching his treasure. - Many delicious foods, gold, jade objects are waiting him to search after. Many essences of philosophy, literature, art, even nature science are waiting him to poss.

In front of him, there may be black and dim, may be bright and brilliant, may be flying rumours, may be blur and dim, may be profound and mystery, may be the cliff and steep, he will pass through without obstacle, through straightly...

The sky is wide for bird to soar, oh, the tiny bird, you do your best to soar what you want, do your best to search what you want!

夜來香

夜來後，花便開了。

這是怎樣的一種花？

為什麼選在夜裡開花？

那花，多麼潔白，又多麼清香！

開放在夜裡，那花有如一盞盞明燈，燃亮在漆漆黑夜裡，花香便是那燦亮的光芒，四處噴灑，無處不在，無孔不入，無邊無際。

開放在夜裡，那花有如一曲曲女高音的歌唱，花香便是那迴腸盪氣的歌音，拔高再拔高，迴盪再迴盪，響遍各處，愉悅人們的聽聞。

開放在夜裡，那花有如一根根插在中流的砥柱，無視於那漫漫逆流橫流急流的衝激鼓盪，誓欲以身殉道，屹然而立，不為所搖，不為所動。

開放在夜裡，那花有如風雨如晦中的雞鳴，不管風雨多大，持續多久，依然不停不歇，始終如一，亙古不變，無所畏懼，予人以警惕，令人警醒。

不去湊熱鬧，不去爭名利，當眾花爭妍鬥艷的白日，它沉默不語，只有當眾花開放過後，落入沉默，不言不語，它才嫣然而笑，盡情綻放，獨芳於暗夜。

是怎樣的一個正人君子！是怎樣的一種貞潔無垢，清香撲鼻的花！

所以，它贏得我深深的敬重和喜愛。

The Tuberose

The flower will open while it's the night.

What kind of flower is it?

Why it picks out the night to open?

How pure white and how pure scent is that flower!

Opens in night, that flower likes a bright lamp one by one, brightening in the darken night, the fragrance is the light from the brilliant radiate, sprinkles everywhere, omnipresent, penetrates into everywhere, boundless.

Opens in the night, that flower likes song soprano one by one, the fragrance is the tune lingering, higher and higher, linger and linger, resounds everywhere, brings happy to all person.

Opens in the night, that flower likes the firm rock in midstream, no looks an eye to the rush agitate of the adverse current, wildly current and rushing current, pledges to die at its post, stands towering, to remain unshaken, to remain unmoved.

Opens in the night, that flower likes the crow of cock in the situation of wind and rain sweeping across a gloomy sky, in spite of how great the wind and rain, how long they last, no stop still, consistently, no change forever, no fear, be vigilant to others, be on the alert to others.

It doesn't to join in fun, doesn't strive after fame and gain. When all flower open in the day for race beauty and gorgeous, it silently no word, just after all the flower opened, and silent, no of any word, it just to appear smile, open at the best, it scents in the dark only.

What a man of noble character he is! What a kind of scent of pure and chaste, assails the nostrils!

Therefore, it obtains my great respect and love!

天堂鳥

是鳥？還是花？假如是鳥，那是怎樣的一種鳥？想必是像鳳凰、麒麟、龍之類生活在傳統裡的動物吧！假如是花，那又是怎樣的一種花？……

向兩側伸展出橘黃色羽毛的雙翅，亭亭而立，彷彿振翅欲飛……哦，欲飛向哪裡？看牠向上翹著一個淡紫色的尖嘴長喙，仰望上方，豈非把目標定在天堂，欲飛向天堂？

是一支銳利的箭，在李廣拉滿了弦的弓上，靜靜地等待著發射，欲脫弦而出？

是一個短跑健將，已經就好了起跑位置，在發令員發出「預備」的口令後，靜靜地等待著那一聲槍聲，欲急衝而出？

靜靜地等待著。這是一種怎樣的姿態？

這是一種嚮往的姿態。

這是一種預備的姿態。

這是一種即將出發的姿態。

靜靜地等待著，牠已經醞釀、磨鍊了多久的時間了？牠的體內已醞釀了多少飛奔急馳的內力了？牠將如何地突破自我、超越自我、提昇自我？……

每次看見牠，我便有一份驚喜，一陣心悸，一種停止呼吸的感覺，總是不敢眨一下眼，怕一眨眼，牠便會從眼前飛逝，留給我一片惆悵……。

The Bird of Paradise Flower

Is it a bird? Is it a flower? What kind of bird is it if it's a bird? Most probably it's a kind of animal like the phoenix, unicorn, dragon in the tradition! And again, what kind of flower is it if it's a flower?

Spreads its orange features to two sides, stands upright, as if it will fly with wields its wings… Er, where will it fly? It lifts upward its purple long sharp bill, look upward, isn't it looks its target at the paradise, want to fly to paradise?

Is it a sharp arrow, on the bow Li Guang fully pull the string, waits silently to be shot, will leave the string to be outward?

Is it a fine sprinter, has taken his place, after the "prepare" is ordered, waits silently the sound of gun, to dash out?

Wait silently. What posture is it?

It's a posture of yearning.

It's a posture of preparation.

It's a posture to be set out.

Wait silently, how long has he brewed and tempered? How many internal force has his body brewed? How will he break through himself, overstep himself, promote himself?…

Every time as I see it, I have a surprise, a palpitation, a feeling of stop breathe, often dare not to blink my eyes, afraid of as soon as one blink, it will fly away from my eyes, leave me a melancholy…

七里香

　　總是彷彿有雨滴在滴落。一朵朵雨花展開五瓣花瓣，在各處盡情地綻放著。每一瓣花瓣寫滿了雪，寫滿了白粉和霜。彷彿有一陣煙帶引花香噴起，噴飛七里，香人鼻息，舒人心胸⋯⋯。

　　是的，雨滴滴落下去。

　　一滴雨是一朵花。

　　兩滴雨是兩朵花⋯⋯。

　　每每，七里香樹成堆成叢地生長在一起，綿延伸展著，枝繁葉茂，綠滿枝稍，建築起一道籬笆。這一道籬笆，由各種角度看，是一條深湛靜流的河，是一片平坦光滑的地板。花就在這籬笆河上綻開，在這籬笆地板上綻開，彷彿是雨滴滴落下去而形成綻開的⋯⋯。

　　一滴雨是一朵花。

　　兩滴雨是兩朵花⋯⋯。

　　雨，不停地滴落，一滴，兩滴⋯⋯。

　　無數雨花不停地綻開，一朵，兩朵⋯⋯。

　　常常，我愛靜立籬畔，靜靜觀賞。

　　那真是雨花呀！一滴滴雨滴落下去，五瓣花瓣便自中心向外反彈而起，向外披展。每一瓣花瓣都是潔白的，彷彿寫滿了雪，寫滿了白粉和霜，彷彿有一陣煙，帶引花香噴起，噴飛七里，香人鼻息，舒人心胸⋯⋯。

　　喜愛七里香。總被七里香所迷。

The Orange Jasmine

It always seems that the raindrop is dripping. The rain flower spreads five petals one after another, blossoms at their best everywhere. Every petal is full written with the snow, full written with the white powder and frost. It seems that a spell of smoke carries flower scent sprinkles, sprinkles to seven li, to assail the nostrils, let me cozy.

Yes. The raindrop is dripping.

A drop of the rain is a flower.

Two drops of the rain are two flowers…

Very often, the orange jasmine trees grow pile up group by group, are stretched continuously, branches and leaves luxuriantly, green full on top of the twig, build a line of fence. From every viewpoint, this line of fence is a river profound and flows silently, a piece of plain and smooth floor. The flowers are blossomed on the fence river, on the fence floor, as if it's formed and blossomed by the dripping of the raindrop.

A drop of the rain is a flower.

Two drops of the rain are two flowers…

The rain drips ceaselessly, one drop, two drop…

Countless rain flowers blossom ceaselessly, one flower, two flowers…

Very often, I stand by the fence silently, appreciate them silently.

It's truly the rain flower! A drop and a drop drip, five petals will bounce outwards from the centre, spread outward. Every petal is pure white, as if they full written the snow, full written the white powder and frost, as if a smoke which carry flower scent sprinkles, sprinkles to seven li, to assail the nostrils, let me cozy.

I love the orange jasmine. I'm often fascinated by the orange jasmine.

春郊

　　春天來了。春天最先來到郊野。它壯盛地來，給郊野添上一份熱鬧。

　　河流由細瘦漸次肥大了起來。它總在陽光下反射出光芒。它因內心興奮而發出的潺潺流水聲，越來越響亮，激濺到各處，瀰漫四方……。

　　樹木脫掉了它們穿得破舊、滯重、灰黃的冬衣，換上了鮮綠輕便的單衣，在風中，在雨裡，在陽光下，顯得那麼活潑、輕快、靈巧，一棵棵像一個個年輕的女孩，輕快地，恣意地，盈盈而笑。

　　鋪在地上那條綠色草坪大毯子，已經換新了，是那麼鮮綠而平坦，柔軟而舒活，茸毛無一脫落或倒伏的，踩上去，便有一股酥軟的感覺從腳底升起。真想躺下去，真想在上面打滾！

　　百花競相綻放，一朵朵，一叢叢，像燈盞，似水晶，噴射出芬芳，展示著萬種顏彩，各種形狀，展示出美……。當然，蜂蝶也來了。牠們穿飛花間，競相賞花採蜜，給花間增加一份熱鬧……。

　　冬眠的動物醒了。看！那不是鼴鼠？那不是蛇、青蛙？……鳥兒也來了，走獸也來了，還有昆蟲也來了。牠們要給春天增加一股熱鬧氣氛，推出一曲交響，吱吱喳喳的，啁啁啾啾的，叮叮鈴鈴的，嘓嘓咯咯的，嗡嗡營營的……。

　　啊，好熱鬧的春郊，請接受我由衷的歌讚！

The Suburb of the Spring

The spring has come. The spring comes to the suburb first. He comes magnificently, adds busy to the suburb.

The river grows fat from thin slowly. He always reflects the radiance under the sunshine. He gurgles due to his exciting in the mind, more and more loudly and clearly, splashes fiercely onto everywhere, permeates in all directions...

The trees take off their worn-out, heavy, grey winter clothes, replace the bright and thin vernal unlined clothes, in the wind, among the rain, under the sunshine, appear active, brisk, dexterous, each tree likes the young girl one and one smile lightly, without restraint.

The great green carpet of the meadow posted on the ground is exchange into the new, how thin and vernal and plane, soft and cozy, the fine hair neither take out nor reverse, step on it, a band of soft feeling arises from the sole of the feet. How really l want to lie down on it! How really I want to roll on it!

All flowers compete to open, one flower after one flower, one tussock after one tussock, like the lamp, like the crystal, spout the fragrance, appear ten thousands of colours, many kinds of form, appear their beauty... Of course, the butterfly and bee comes also. They fly through the flowers, and gather the honey, add the busy to the flowers.

The hibernate animal is awaken. Lo, is it not the mole? Is it not the serpent, the frog? And there comes the bird also, there comes the beast also, and the insect still. They add an air of busy to the spring, push forward a tune of symphony, creak and chirrup, chirp and twitter, jingle and jingle, hum and hum...

Oh, what a busy suburb it is, welcome my eulogize please!

春情

　　不像少女的，至少也像少男的。

　　有時候，一大早心情就不好，也不知為什麼，反正就是悶悶不樂，鬱鬱寡歡。看他情況有異，趨前好心慰問，招來一頓白眼還算是好的，有時惹來一頓臭罵。待事過境遷，問他何故那樣？他竟張大口，沒話好說。原來他自己也鬧不清！

　　有時候，好端端的，和人家有說有笑，融洽無間；只因為一句話，他突然放聲號啕大哭，淚流滿面；沒幾分鐘，嘿，又好了，又是有說有笑了。

　　也會覺得身上奇怪，好像肌肉或骨骼會有痠痛之感，但不久又好了。

　　也會突然覺得自己好像長大了，做什麼事都要老陳熟練，蠻像個大人，卻又突然天真活潑起來，言行舉止有如小孩，有時候讓人說成大人，有時候又被人說成小孩。到底是大人或小孩，不僅別人，連他自己也搞得暈頭轉向。

　　也常常有著幻想，有著對異性愛的嚮往，並且敏感異常，動不動就臉紅。

　　總之，時冷時熱，時好時壞，時喜時悲……。

　　據說這就是春情，常常是很尷尬的，常常是混沌的。

　　據說這是生理影響心理的結果。

　　就會漸漸長成熟的。就會漸漸趨於穩定的。就會成為過去的。……

The Spring Emotion

At least a boyhood if it isn't a girlhood.

Sometimes his emotion isn't good in the early morning, doesn't know why, in any case it's stifling, smouldering. As he looks like unusual, tends to convey greetings, provoke a cold stare is the best, sometimes has a scold mercilessly still. After it's over, ask why he does, he is agape and tongue-tied, no word to respond. He can't make clear himself originally.

Sometimes when he everything is all right, talking and laughing with others, on friendly terms; he cries loudly suddenly just for one word, tears cover his face; for a few minute, hey, nice again, turns back to talking and laughing again.

And also feels strange in the body, as if it feels pain in his muscle and skeleton, but fine again soon.

Also feels it looks like grown up suddenly, seasoned experienced and capable in managing business, looks quite like an adult, but back to innocent and vivacious suddenly again, looks like a child in words and deeds as well as manner, sometimes to be defined an adult, and sometimes to be defined a child. In the final, is he an adult or a child? not only the others but also himself is dizzy.

He often has the illusion, has the wish to the love of opposite sex, and too sensitive, blushes very often.

About all, now cold now warm, now fine now bad, now pleasure now sad...

It's said it's the spring emotion, often it's awkward, often it's chaos.

It's said it's the result of the physiology influence the psychology.

It will be ripen slowly. It will be tended to steady slowly. It will be over.

春的訊息

　　日復一日，春的訊息傳了過來，由遠而近，由淡而濃，由稀疏而繁密……

　　最早擔任傳遞工程的是偶來的暖日。在寒冬裡，只要它一來，便頻頻送出陽光的微笑，化成一堆堆火苗，揮發出溫暖，融去寒凍。

　　漸漸地，自願擔任傳遞工作的，越來越多，越來越踴躍了……

　　芽苗，有的在泥土裡，有的在枝幹上，摸索了不知多久，穿過黑暗，穿過孤寂，穿過寒冷，終於突現了出來，驚喜地傳遞出一份春的訊息。

　　而這一份春的訊息，由白白嫩嫩起，由稀稀疏疏起，漸次濃密起來，漸次幻化成綠，由淺綠而淡綠而濃綠，宛然成枝成葉，成草成樹，成叢成片成群，源源而出，不絕如縷……

　　流水在河裡，漸次泛漲出春的訊息……

　　天空中，空氣裡，也傳遞著春的訊息。那是越來越晴朗的天氣，越來越溫暖的春風，越來越響亮的蟲鳥鳴唱，越來越明亮的陽光……

　　而春的訊息終於綻開成花，多彩多姿，多種多樣，而又清香撲鼻……

　　春的訊息繼續傳遞著，日復一日，漸漸地，由近而遠，由濃而淡，由繁密而稀疏……

The Message of the Spring

One day after another day, the message of the spring passes on, from far to near, from weak to dense, from thin to thick…

The earliest transmitter is the warm day passes on by chance. In the chill winter, as long as it passes on, it will send the smile of the sunshine repeatedly, and turns into a pile and a pile of fire sign, gives vent to warmth, drives away the chill.

The one who bears the work of pass on, are more and more in number, more and more vie with one another slowly.

The buds, some are under the soil, some are on the branches and twigs, I don't know how long it fumbled, passed through the dark, passed through the solitude, passed through the chill, it appeared suddenly at the end, passed on a piece of the message of the spring with pleasant surprise.

And this piece message of the spring, bases on the white and tender, bases on the sparsity, grows thick and dense slowly, turns illusorily into green, from light green into weak green slowly, as if they come to branches and leaves, to grasses to trees, to tussocks to pieces and groups, incessantly, hanging by a thread…

The water in the river goes up the message of the spring slowly…

On the sky, in the air, there passes on the message of the spring also. Those are the finer of the weather, the warmer of the spring wind, the louder of the song of the birds and insects, the brighter of the sunshine.

And the message of the spring blossoms into flowers, colourful and postures, diversities and also fragrance assails the nostrils.

The message passes on successively, one day after another day, from near to far, from dense to weak, from thick to thin slowly…

畫春

　　這個小女孩在畫春。她一次次調著顏彩，右手拿著畫筆，一次次去沾水彩，在畫紙上畫著，要把春的面貌畫下來，讓春永遠留駐。

　　是春了。春是多麼美好呀！

　　微風輕輕吹來，以她特有輕緩柔軟的纖纖玉手，輕輕撫弄著樹，輕輕撫弄著花，輕輕撫弄著草，輕輕撫弄著人們，尤其是輕輕撫弄著這個小女孩的長髮，撫弄得髮絲絲絲飄揚空際……。

　　從晴朗的天空，陽光不停地噴灑而下。那是細碎的金粉玉屑，成群結隊，到處盈滿，噴灑得到處亮晃晃的，溫暖暖的。

　　芽兒滋長了，然後是葉子……。

　　是白如意，然後是嫩黃玉，然後是綠珠串……。

　　綠珠串，綠珠串，綠珠串……綠珠串終於盈滿整個大地了。

　　當然，花兒也開放了。那是點綴珠串的顏色，這裡一簇那裡一叢地……生動多了，富變化多了。是顏彩繽紛了。

　　她揮著筆畫著，想把這些畫進去，並且想把人們也畫進去。他們是用自己在畫春的呢。

　　其實，我也在畫。我畫她所畫的以及她。

　　想想，是她畫的是春還是我畫的才是春？

Painting the spring

The girl is painting the spring. She blends the colours, time and again, holds the paint brush on her right hand, painting on the paper, tries to paint the image of the spring, leaves the spring forever.

It's the spring. How fine is the spring!

The breeze blows gently, with her special soft released tiny hands, touches the tree slightly, touches the flower slightly, touches the grass slightly, touches the people slightly, especially touches the long hairs of this girl slightly, touches the thread of the hairs fluttering in the air...

The sunshine sprinkles ceaselessly from the clear sky. It's the fine golden powder and jade filing, in groups and in large numbers, full of everywhere, sprinkles fully everywhere into twinkling, sufficient warmth.

There are in bud first, and then the leaves...

It's the white scepter first, then the tender jade, then the green pearl string...

The green pearl string, the green pearl string, the green pearl string... the green pearl string sprinkles fully whole the earth.

Of course, the flower blossoms also. That is the colour to adorn the pearl string, here is a cluster there is a tussock... more vivid, more changeable. It's in riotous profusion.

She wields the paint brush to paint, try to paint these into the picture, and also paint the people into the picture. They paint the spring by themselves.

In fact, I'm also painting. I paint she painted and her.

Guess, does she painted is the spring or I painted is?

與春對話

——春姑娘，妳好！好久不見了。妳匆匆忙忙地，上哪兒？

——到處走走。

——到處走走，幹嘛？

——趕走冬，趕走寒冷和枯萎，給大家帶溫暖來。

——那可好！

——還有，睽違一年了，我要去拜訪那些老朋友，樹木和花草。

——他們怎樣？

——他們應該和去年一樣，發芽，長葉，開花……。

——還拜訪誰？

——還拜訪鳥獸、昆蟲，尤其是那隻可愛的小白兔。

——他們有什麼好拜訪的？

——看他們跑、跳，聽他們叫、唱，就覺得很快樂。

——妳是從哪裡來的？

——從很遠很遠的地方來的。

——過去一年裡，妳到哪兒去了？

——我到處嬉遊，欣賞美麗的風景。

——看到了很多？

——是呀！看到了很多。

——妳對將來如何打算？

——我還是要到處走走，到處嬉遊……。

Dialogue with the Spring

–Miss Spring, how do you do! Haven't seen you for a long time. You're in a hurry, where are you going?

–Just take a walk to everywhere.

–For what you take a walk to everywhere?

–Drive the winter, drive the chill and wither, and bring the warmth for all.

–It's good.

–Besides, separate for a year, I will like to visit the old friends, trees and flowers and grasses.

–What do they about?

–They ought to be the same as last year: sprout, putting forth leaves, blossoming...

–And whom else you will visit?

–Besides, I'll visit the birds, animals, insects, especially the lovely bunny.

–How are they worth you to visit?

–I feel very happy while seeing them on run, jump, hearing from them on call, sing.

–Where do you come from?

–I come from the place faraway.

–Where did you live this year?

–I go to take a tour, to appreciate the landscape.

–Have you seen many things?

–Yes. I saw many things.

–How do you plan for the future?

–I still will take a walk everywhere, and take a tour everywhere...

與春同在

　　春來了。我與春同在。

　　與春同在，一切醜陋沒有了，所有的都是美麗的；一切煩惱沒有了，所有的都是心平氣和的；一切不安沒有了，所有的都是寧靜的；一切邪惡都沒有了，所有的都是純潔的……。

　　在春裡，草木欣欣向榮，相互比賽著，看誰長得比較青，長得比較綠，長得比較高大。與春同在，我便享有這些青綠，這些欣欣向榮。

　　在春裡，百花競相綻放，呈出千彩，呈出所有的美，把大地裝點得風光明媚。與春同在，我便享有這些千彩，這些美，這些明媚風光。

　　在春裡，昆蟲和眾鳥大展歌喉，盡情地歌唱，歌唱出欣喜、婉轉的歌音。與春同在，我便享有這些歌，這些欣喜。

　　在春裡，和風吹撫在人身上，暖陽照拂在人身上，送出舒適、溫暖和光明。與春同在，我便享有這些和風，這些暖陽，這些舒適，這些溫暖，這些光明。

　　在春裡，一切都甦醒過來了，一切都振作起來了，一切都愉快起來了，一切都活潑起來了。與春同在，我便享有這些甦醒，這些振作，這些愉悅，這些活潑。

　　春來了。我與春同在。

　　與春同在，就有滿滿的春，沒有炎熱的夏、蕭瑟的秋、酷冷的冬了。

Get Together with the spring

The spring has come. I get together with spring.

Get together with spring, all ugly are vanished, all are beautiful; all trouble are vanished, all are in a calm state of mind; all uneasy are vanished, all are peace; all evil are vanished, all are pure…

In the spring, grass and tree are flourishing, compare with each other, who is the more vernal, who is the greener, who is the taller. Get together with spring, I enjoy these verdant and green, these flourishing.

In the spring, all flowers compare to blossom, present thousands of colour, present all beauty, adorn the earth into scenery. Get together with spring, I enjoy these thousands of colour, these beauties, these scenery.

In the spring, the insects and birds fully display their singing, sing their best, sing out their pleasant, the wind tune. Get together with spring, I enjoy these songs, these pleasant.

In the spring, the breeze touches on the body of the people, the warm sunshine touches on the body of the people, presents the cozy, warmth and brilliance. Get together with spring, I enjoy the breeze, the warm sunshine, the cozy, the warmth, the brilliance.

In the spring, all are revived, all are brace themselves up, all are pleasant, are vivid. Get together with spring, I enjoy these revive, these brace up, these pleasant, these vivid.

Spring has come. I get together with spring.

Get together with spring, there's but fully spring, not the hot summer, desolate autumn and chill winter.

炮竹花

期待好久好久了，炮竹花提起腳跟，伸長頸項，站立如企鵝，期待春天的來臨，在路旁，在田野，在花園，在人間……。

當春天哼著她的歌，捏弄著她的衣角，緩步而來，炮竹花便劈劈啪啪地拍著手──拍紅了手，拍紅了臉，滿臉堆著笑，歡欣鼓舞地迎接著她的來臨，在路旁，在田野，在花園，在人間……。

那是怎樣的一種美景！幾個孩子搗著耳朵，顯現畏怯的樣子，臉上掛著天真。一個孩子拿著點燃的香條，伸長手去點燃炮竹，遂有劈啪之聲響起，有漫空輕煙，有孩子搗著耳朵……。

然後，搗著耳朵的手放下了……。

然後，一個個孩子的臉綻滿花朵了……。

然後，當然是一串串炮竹花，一串串春天了……。

其實，炮竹花何嘗不是春天？不是在歡唱春天的歌？拍手本身就捏弄得出春天來，就在歡唱春天的歌！從掌心可以拍出一個春來，唱出一個春天來……。

一串拍起，一串拍起，又一串拍起……。

一串唱起，一串唱起，又一串唱起……。

一串拍起，一串唱起，擠擠挨挨，是一片紅的海，洋溢一片紅彩，一片歡顏，一片童趣，一片春景……。

啊，炮竹花，紅彩，歡顏，童趣，春景……。

Fire-cracker Vine

Awaiting for long time, the fire-cracker vine stands like penguin with tiptoe, extends his neck, hoping the coming of the spring, by the road, in the field, in the garden, in the world…

When the spring comes slowly with singing, twists the hem of his dress, the fire-cracker vine will clap his hands, - claps into red his hands, claps into red his face, piles fully his smile, to welcome joyfully at her coming, by the road, in the field, in the garden, in the world…

What it's a kind of beautiful landscape! There are some boys with naïve; on their face, cowardly covers their ears. One of them takes a joss stick in burning, stretches his hand to ignite the fire-cracker, so that there sound the claps, the thin smoke fills whole the sky, and there are the boys cover their ears…

Then, the hands cover the ears put down…

Then, there blossoms fully on every boy's face…

Then, of course there are cluster and cluster of fire-cracker vine, cluster and cluster of spring…

In fact, is it not the spring the fire-crack vine? Is it not the song sung joyfully of the spring? Clap hands originally can twist out the spring, can sing out joyfully the song of spring! A spring can be clapped out from the centre of the palm, and sung out from the centre of the palm…

Clap a cluster, clap a cluster, and clap cluster again…

Sing a cluster, sing a cluster, and sing a cluster…

Clap a cluster, sing a cluster, huddle together, it's a stretch of red sea, is permeated fully with a stretch of red colour, a stretch of joyful face, a stretch of children's delight…

Oh, fire-crack vine, red colour, joyful face, children's delight, and spring landscape…

報春花

「春天來了。」每到春天，時刻一到，報春花便會為大家報告春來的消息。

報春花為大家報告春來的消息，每年如此，從不間斷，以它們的葉，以它們的花……。

「春天來了。」報春花揚舉著葉，以它們的葉報告春來的消息。看，它們像一面旗，更鮮綠了，更有生氣了，更精神抖擻了。

報春花為大家報告春來的消息，每年如此，從不間斷，以它們的葉，以它們的花……。

「春天來了。」報春花高擎起花，以它們的花報告春來的消息。看，它們的花，紅、橙、黃、藍、紫、紫紅……各色都有，點著頭，有的僅綻放一朵小小的微笑，有的則開懷地放聲大笑。

報春花為大家報告春來的消息，每年如此，從不間斷，以它們的葉，以它們的花……。

萬物應和著，迎了上去，那些鳥和鳴蟲以歌唱，那些花草樹木以新芽、綠葉和花朵，那些走獸以蹦躍奔馳，那些鳥、蝴蝶和青蜓以飛翔，那些泥土以濕潤，那些天氣以溫暖，那些空氣以春風……。

「春天來了。」每到春天，時刻一到，報春花便會為大家報告春來的消息，每年如此，從不間斷，以它們的葉，以它們的花……。

Chinese Primrose

"The spring is coming." The Chinese primrose reports for us about the news of the spring whenever the spring comes.

The Chinese primrose reports for us about the news of spring, so every year, haven't broken, with their leaves, with their flowers…

"The spring is coming." The Chinese primrose high lifts their leaves, reports about the news of the spring. Lo, they like the flag, is more vivid green, is more with vigour and vitality, is more in good fettle.

The Chinese primrose reports for us about the news of spring, so every year, haven't broken, with their leaves, with their flowers…

"The spring is coming." The Chinese primrose high lift their flowers, reports about the news of the spring. Lo, their flowers, red, orange, yellow, blue, purple, purple red… all colour they have, nodding, some just blossom a little smile, and some laugh a hearty laugh.

The Chinese primrose reports for us about the news of spring, so every year, haven't broken, with their leaves, with their flowers…

Echo all things of the world, face on, those singing birds and chirp insects, with their song, those flowers, grasses and trees with their bud, green leaves and flowers, the beast with their jumping and running, those birds, butterflies and dragonflies with their soar, those soil with their moist, those weather with their warm, those air with their spring wind…

"The spring is coming." The Chinese primrose reports for us about the news of spring, so every year, haven't broken, with their leaves, with their flowers…

春天球戲

冬天過去了。春天來了。春寒料峭。

這樣的天氣,對一個血壓低、怕冷的我來說,雖然春光爛然,我寧可不外出,窩在書房看書,咀嚼書中美味,挖掘書中寶藏。

上午約九時,正當我沉浸在書海中,要享書中日月長,外面傳來了一群小孩子的叫喊聲:

「好球!」……「壞球!」……「安打,哈,二壘安打!」……「三振出局!」……「接殺出局!」……「好!滑壘成功!」……「快跑!加油!……哇,被封殺了!」……「兩出局了!」……「沒關係!來兩個全壘打!……對!用力!可能全壘打喔!……哇,真的全壘打!真好!我們贏了!」……

我想他們一定是在玩一場精彩的棒球賽。由他們的叫聲聽來,他們玩得很熱鬧呢。

叫喊聲繼續傳來,叫喊聲越來越大,越來越熱烈,越來越熱鬧,終於把我引到了窗邊。

窗前出現了一片奇景:一、二十個小孩子,在窗前不遠的空地上,玩著打棒球遊戲。戴著手套的,拿著棒子的,當裁判的……各就各位。球在投手和捕手之間來回著,有時被打出去……。即使春寒料峭,仍有一半以上小孩子脫去了上衣,大家生龍活虎地奔跑、跳躍、喊叫……

啊,玩吧!鬧吧!成長吧!春天本來就是屬於小孩子的。

The Ball Game of the Spring

The winter is over. The spring is coming. The spring chill is chilly.

As to a person low pressure of blood and afraid of the cold like me, in thus a weather, though it's splendour of spring, I would rather to nest indoor instead of going outdoor and read book in the study room to chew the flavour of the books, dig out the treasure of the books.

About 9 of the forenoon, when I sink in the book sea to enjoy the long day, there circulate the shouting of a group of the children:

"Strike!"... "Ball!"... "Take base! Ha, two base hit!"... "Struck-out!"... "Put out!"... "Good! Sliding!"... "Fast run hurry up! Make a greater effort!... Woe, force out!"... "Two out!"... "Never mind! Having two home run!... It's right! Be straining! May be a home run!... Oh, really the home run! Really good! We win." ...

I think they are playing a splendid baseball game. They play into bustling from their shout.

There circulates the sound of the shouting continually, the sound of the shouting is louder and louder, and ardent and bustling, and leads me to the window at last.

In front of the window, there appears a wonderful sight: about ten or twenty children play baseball game on the empty space no far near the window. Some wear the globe, some hold the bat, may some be the umpire... They all take their place. The ball back and forth between pitcher and catcher, sometimes be hit by the batter... Even the spring chill is chilly, it still a half of the children take off their upper outer garment, all of them run, jump, and shout lively as a dragon or a tiger...

Oh, playing! Bustling! Grow up! The spring is belonged to children originally.

花季

　　春日裡，花季到了。

　　花季，花開的季節，眾花競相以身體的語言作自我表現的季節！

　　桃、李、杏、櫻、杜鵑、水仙、木蘭、玫瑰、羊蹄甲、一串紅、紫羅蘭、蒲公英……哇，好多種花呀，好多朵呀！它們，或成蕾，或含苞，或微綻，或盛開，在春風中輕輕搖曳，在春陽下閃發光芒，集朵成串，成簇，成叢，展現視覺的美，有紅色的，有白色的，有黃色的，有紫色的，有灑金的……各色都有，且各色又各自有深淺，配置勻稱，有如一個個婀娜美女，展露笑靨，穿紅著綠，輕移蓮步，舞姿曼妙，散發出或濃或淡的芳香，真是名副其實的「花團錦簇」、「花枝招展」！

　　從花園起，這些花，朵朵，串串，簇簇，叢叢，開向庭院、田野、平原、高山、水邊，開向陽台、樓頂、盆景、家屋客廳，開向人間……。

　　它們很是豁達，願將所有分享天下。無論哪裡，它們都會分贈出美麗、芳香、笑容、快樂、慈祥、和諧、幸福……。

　　每個人也應該是一朵花，心胸豁達，願將所有分享天下。無論到哪裡，他總和別人融洽相處，共同組成燦麗的花園，擁有並分贈出美麗、芳香、笑容、快樂、慈祥、和諧、幸福……。

The Blossom

As soon as the spring is here, the blossom is here.

Blossom, the season of the flower opens, multitudinous flower compares to express themselves with the language of the body.

Peach, plum, apricot, cherry, azalea, narcissus, lily magnolia, rose, orchid tree, fire-cracker vine, violet, dandelion… wow, there are many kinds of flower, there are many pieces of flower! May they be flower bud, may they be bud, may they be faint open, may they be wide open, all sway slightly in the vernal wind, shining under the spring sun, for piece, for cluster, for bunch, for tussock, unfold before our eyes the beauty of sense of sight, some are red, some are white, some are yellow, some are purple, some are gold-sprinkling… have all colour, and have deep and shadow on every colour, well-balanced, like one and one belle, appear the smile face, wear red and green, step their tiny steps slightly, the posture is splendid, sprinkles fragrance dense or thin, in really as well as in name "gorgeous spectacle" and "in showy dress".

Begin from the garden, these flowers, piece and piece, cluster and cluster, bunch and bunch, tussock and tussock, blossom to courtyard, field, plain, mountain, waterside, blossom to balcony, the top of the mansion, potted landscape, house, reception room, blossom to world…

They are very open-minded, willing to share all of themselves to everyone. Wherever they are, they will gift to others the beauty, fragrance, smile, joy, benign harmony and happy…

Everybody ought to be a flower, open-minded, willing to share all of themselves to everyone. Wherever he is, he will gift to others the beauty, fragrance, smile, joy, benign, harmony and happy…

在暖春裡

寒冬走了。暖春來了。哇，多麼美好！

走了，都走了，那些和寒冬在一起的。走了，都走了，那些寒風冷雨，那些枯槁零落，那些憂鬱疾苦。走了，都走了！

宇宙萬有顯得生氣蓬勃。太陽光更加明亮、溫暖了，把各處照耀得燦爛輝煌。晴空萬里，蔚藍亮麗，彷彿塗上了一層薄蠟。到處有草木的芽葉在突長，像雨後春筍，探頭探腦地，有些紅嫩如剛生下來嬰兒的肌膚，有些白嫩如象牙，慢慢滋長轉化成淡綠、濃綠，有花朵綻放，吒紫嫣紅，爭美鬥豔。蛙、蛇、土撥鼠等等冬眠的動物甦醒過來了，又恢復活動了。鴨、鵝游向水中央，悠悠自在。牛、羊在草原吃草。野生動物到處奔逐。蟲、鳥放開了喉嚨，唱出巧囀美妙的歌，也放開舞步，瘋狂地舞蹈。到處好熱鬧。

人逢喜事精神爽。外界事務之影響一個人，是相當大的。在暖春裡，我們怎能只是眼睜睜地看著草木蓬勃生長，百花齊放，蟲鳥爭鳴、狂舞，野獸奔逐？

那麼，讓我們活動起來吧！不要瑟縮地侷處在一個角落裡！我們要勇敢地走出屋外，遠離陰鬱、枯槁，輕快地走向郊野、高山、海邊，去踏青、露營，享受春天贈予的盛宴，去研讀大自然這本大書，呼吸新鮮的空氣，沐浴在燦爛的陽光中，獲得智慧、健康、快樂和美。

寒冬走了。暖春來了。啊，多麼美好！

In the Warm Spring

Chilly winter is gone. Warm spring is coming. Wow, how fine it is!

Is gone, all is gone those together with winter. Is gone, all is gone those chilly wind and cold rain, those withered and declined, those melancholies and sufferings. Gone, all is gone!

All beings in the universe appear full with life. More bright and more warmth the sunshine, illumines everywhere brilliant. Clear and boundless sky, azure and brilliance, as if smeared a layer of feeble wax. There are sprouted of the grasses and trees sticking out, like spring shoots after the rain, pop their heads in and look about, some soft red as the skin of the baby just born, some soft white like elephant's tusk, grow slowly and turn into light green, thick green, some flowers blossoming, gorgeous purple and bright red, contend for strange and gorgeous. The hibernated animals like frog, serpent, marmot etc. are awakened, resume movement again. Duck, goose swims to the center of the water, leisurely and freely. Cattle, goat chews grasses on the grassland. Undomesticated animals run and chase. Insects and birds lift their throat to sing the winding fine song, and set their dancing step, dancing wildly. It's very bustling!

One will in high spirits when he has a happy event. It makes great influence to a person the thing from outside. In the warm spring, how can we unfeelingly with wide open eyes of the grasses and trees grow vigorously, all flowers blossom together, insects and birds contend in singing, wide dancing, undomesticated animals run and chase?

Then, let's actively! Don't huddle ourselves to be confined in a corner. We must go outdoor bravely far free from the melancholy and withered, go briskly toward suburb, mountain, seaside, for outing, bivouac, to enjoy the grand banquet spring gift, to research the grand book of the nature, breathe the fresh air, bath in the brilliant sunshine, obtain wisdom, healthiness, joy and beauty.

Chilly winter is gone. Warm spring is coming. Wow, how fine it is!

羊蹄甲

　　羊蹄甲，又叫紫荊？香港櫻花？印度櫻花？管它們是什麼名稱，只要每年帶來春就好了。名稱只是個記號，抽象地代表一個人或一件事物而已。有什麼好計較的？

　　零散的，成群的，在校園，在路旁，在花園，它們站立著，撐開一把大傘，布篷上綴著一朵朵中間深紫漸向外緣漸次淡紫的花。不管盛放或微放，一朵羊蹄甲便是一個春字。

　　是的，一朵羊蹄甲便是一個春字。既如此，那麼，一樹羊蹄甲便是一樹春字了。啊，春在枝頭！春由羊蹄甲帶來，燦爛人間！

　　豈僅是「紅杏枝頭春意鬧」？豈僅是「桃李爭春」？春，豈僅是以櫻花、杜鵑來代表？以鶯飛草長來代表？羊蹄甲不讓它們專美於前，更是春的使者，春的化身。

　　它們總是先開花後長葉的。

　　在初春，它們便開出花來了。在料峭的春風中，紫色花瓣不住飄搖著，令人聯想到，那是一隻隻紫色的蝴蝶，馱著春，停在枝頭，欲飛不飛，翅膀一張一合，將春意撒布人間，將春意攪濃。

　　然後，葉子長出來了。多麼奇妙！它的葉子，一葉葉竟然是一個個羊蹄模印。是哪一隻神羊給踩印出來的？……一定是春之神羊了！

　　管它是什麼名稱，只要每年帶來春就好了。

The Orchid Tree

Orchid tree, is it also called redbud, and also called Hong Kung orchid tree, or India cherry blossom? No matter what name it is, it's enough only it can carry spring. The name is a score, just represents abstractly a person or a thing. What will be concerned for?

Be scattered, be in group, in the campus, by the roadside, in the garden, they halt, open a big umbrella, there dot slowly one by one the flower from inner to edge the shade purple to the light purple. No matter it's grand open or slight open, an orchid tree is a spring.

Yes, an orchid tree is a spring. Since it is, then, a tree of flower is a tree of spring. Oh, the spring is on the branch. Spring is carried by the orchid tree, to give brilliance to the world.

Is it just "the red apricot bustle the breath of spring"? Is it just "the peach and plum strive to be the first to do the spring"? Is spring just represented by cherry and azalea? Is spring just represented by oriole fly and grass luxuriant? Orchid tree wouldn't let them to be beauty monopolize, it's more be the angel of spring, the personification of spring.

They blossom first and then putting forth leaves.

They blossom in early spring. The purple petals swinging in the chill wind, let us to deem they are the butterflies one by one, carry the spring, stop on the branches, haven't fly as if to fly, in turn to stretch and close the wings, scatter the breath of spring to the world, stir thick the breath of spring.

Then it puts forth the leaves. How strange it is! Every leave is one and one of the hoof seal of the goat unexpectedly. Is it which god goat treaded?... It must be the god goat of spring!

In spite of what the name it is, just it carries spring every year is enough.

春晨

　　春天是一年裡最美好的季節，早晨是一天中最美好的時刻。它們同樣受人們讚美、歡迎。春晨是一年裡最美好的季節中的一天中最美好的時刻，其受人極度讚美、歡迎，自不在話下了。

　　在春天裡，天氣是溫暖的，太陽總撒出一片光明來。春雷響了，驚蟄了，鼴鼠、青蛙、蟲、蛇等冬眠的動物都紛紛出洞了。河水漲了。草兒盡情地綠，像一片綠火在燃燒，一直蔓延開去。樹青了，青向天際，青向樹梢。繁花競相綻放，像在比賽看誰開得美，開得嬌，開得香，鳥兒、蟲子儘量地鳴唱，也是在比賽，看誰的最好聽，誰的聲音最大……。

　　雞啼了。夜去了。早晨來了。所有的黑暗盡去。光明已經降臨大地。所有的汙濁已經盡去。到處是一片清新。所有的疲憊已經盡去。萬物甦醒過來了，充滿了活力。所有的憂傷已經盡去。欣悅充滿各處，充滿萬物的臉上、心內。啊，在早晨裡，有多少光明，多少清新，多少欣悅！

The Vernal Morning

The spring is the best season of a year. The morning is the best moment of a day. They both are praised and welcomed by the people. Vernal morning is the best moment of a day of the best season, of course, it's nothing to say that it's praised and welcomed extremely by the people.

The weather is warm in the spring. The sun always sprinkles a scene of brilliance. The spring thunder is sounded, insect is awakened, come out from the hole one after another the hibernated animals, the mole, frog, insect and serpent etc. The river water is rose. The grass greened at their best, like a scene of green fire burning, and burning continuously. The tree is green, green toward the azure, green toward the top of the tree. Complicated flowers are opened fiercely, like in contend who is the most beautiful, open to be delicate and charming the most, open to be fragrance the most, and the birds, the insects singing their best, also contend whose sound is the best to listen, whose sound is the loudest…

The cock is crowed. The night is gone. The morning is come. Whole the dark is gone. The brilliance is fallen on the earth. Whole the dirty is gone. There is fresh everywhere. Whole the tired is gone. Ten thousand of things are awakened, full of vitality. There gone whole the sad. There fills everywhere the pleasure, and also the face, the inner of heart. Oh, in the morning, how many brilliance is here, how many fresh is here, how many pleasure is here!

春光如酒

那個上午，我在窗下坐讀，原本全心沉浸在書中，忘懷身外物的；一定是哪個軟物撞上窗玻璃撞得太重了，竟然能使我分神從書頁間抬起頭來察看。

原來是一隻烏嘴鵯仔。牠飛行時不小心，撞上了窗玻璃，昏厥在地。所幸不久牠就醒轉過來飛走了。

這是為什麼？是牠想飛下來和我共讀嗎？為什麼這麼糊塗？為什麼沒注意到窗玻璃？……

這麼想著，我沒心情繼續坐讀下去了。

我站了起來，走出屋外……。

一走出屋外，我頓時了悟了。

原來是春光如酒，牠被春光的醇酒所深深沉醉了。

大地間的萬物，醺醺然沉醉著，在春光的醇酒裡。

那些花草樹木，枝枝沉醉，葉葉醺然，花花酣暢，在微風中，展現各種美姿，各種顏彩，展現紛繁，也搖曳，也歡舞，醉態嫵媚。

那些昆蟲，尤其是蝴蝶、蜜蜂，衝著群花，不住地飛，不住地舞，發狂地飛，發狂地舞，醉得迷迷糊糊，醉眼矇矓，不省人事，七顛八倒，亂闖亂撞……。

那些鳥，一定也是喝醉了。牠們大聲地鳴，盡情地唱，把歌聲傳向各處，任其紛飛……。

這時，我也沉醉在春天的醇酒裡了。

我但願能常時沉醉其中，不再醒來！

As the Wine Splendour of Spring

I take a seat in front of the window that forenoon, am indulging in the book whole my mind originally, forget myself; it must be which soft body dash against the windowpane too heavy, make me raise my head to search it from my attention on the book page.

It's a scaly-breast munia originally. He flies with carelessly, dashes the window pane, and goes off in a faint. He wakes up very soon luckily and flies away.

Why is it? Is he going to fly to read with me together? Why is he so puzzle? Why does he take no attention of the windowpane?...

Thus thinking, I am not in the mood for reading in sitting here continuously.

I stand up, and go outdoors.

I suddenly realized as soon as I go outdoors.

It as like as the wine splendour of spring originally, he is deep intoxicated with the rich wine of splendour of spring.

Everything in the world, are drunken with intoxicated, in the splendour of spring.

Those flowers, grasses and trees, intoxicated every twig, drunken every leave, drinks to its heart's content every flower, appear their beautiful posture in the breeze, appear numerous and complicated of every colour, also swing, also dance joyfully, coquetry the drunkenness.

Those insects, especially the butterflies, honeybees, charge the flowers, fly and dance ceaselessly, fly madly, dance madly, are dead intoxicated in faint, dim their drunken eyes, unconsciously, topsy-turvy, in confusion to strike and dash...

Those birds, must drunken also. They chirp loudly, sing to their heart's content, deliver the song toward everywhere, flutter as they please.

I'm also intoxicated in the wine splendour of spring.

Just wish I can always intoxicate within, and never awaken again!

春·蝶舞

　　眾蝴蝶飛舞著，在空中……。

　　這是最美好的季節：春天。這是最美好的時間：上午九點左右。這是最美好的天氣：晴天。三個最美好相乘相加，哇，三倍或三乘方的最美好！

　　太陽是大公無私的。它把它的金粉普遍而均勻地撒滿各地，給出光明和溫暖……。

　　春風到處雲遊著，以其特有柔軟的手，送出溫情。空氣中蘊含著一種沁透人心肺的涼爽……。

　　土地的蘊藏極富，正發揮其巨力……。

　　植物欣欣向榮。許多花、草、樹木或伸出嫩芽和嫩葉，或開出花朵，散發它們的芳香……。

　　眾蝴蝶就在這中間飛舞著……。

　　飛舞呀飛舞！牠們穿著各種顏色的華美舞衣，忽上忽下，忽左忽右，忽疾忽徐，忽來忽去，穿進穿出，身影款擺著，應和著一定的韻律節奏，正向，反向，斜向，翻轉，旋動，展現優美的舞姿……。

　　牠們是什麼蝴蝶？鳳蝶？小蛺蝶？木葉蝶？斑蝶？灰蝶？……

　　牠們跳的什麼舞？勃魯斯？華爾滋？恰恰？芭蕾？……古典舞？民族舞？現代舞？……

　　牠們飛舞著，在某一個晴朗的春天上午九點左右，在三種最美好的相乘相加裡……。

The Butterfly Dancing in the Spring

There are multitudinous butterflies dancing in the air…

This is the best season of the year: Spring. This is the best time: about 9 o'clock forenoon. This is the best weather: fine day. Three best plus in one, wow, the best with triple or the power of three.

The sun is selfless. It sprinkles golden powder everywhere commonly and equally, sends out the brilliance and warmth…

Vernal wind tours free high in the clouds, with its special soft hands, sends out the warmth. There contains a kind of cool penetrates the whole body…

It's extreme rich the contain of the soil, and is playing the role of its great power…

The plant is flourishing. Many of the flower, grass and tree stretch their buds and leaves, or blossom, spread their fragrance.

There are multitudinous butterflies dancing among them.

They dancing and dancing! They wear the dancing splendid clothing of variant cloud, now up now down, now right now left, now quick now slow, now forth now back, now in now out, posture is excellent, respond with certain meter and rhythm, forward, backward, inclined ward, turn down, revolve, appear the beautiful dancing posture…

What kind of butterfly are they? Is it papiliandae? Kallimainachus? Milk weed? Lycaenidae? Grey butterfly?…

What kind of dance do they play? Is it bluesy? Waltz? Cha cha? Ballet?… classical dancing? Folk dance? Modern dance?…

They are dancing, at about 9 forenoon of a certain fine day, the best with triple or the power of three.

晨鳥鳴唱

晨鳥鳴唱著，在窗外，在樹上，在田野⋯⋯

晨鳥鳴唱著，要唱走黑夜，唱來白天⋯⋯。

在整個宇宙間，最忠誠於「早睡早起」的，可能是除了貓頭鷹以外的所有鳥類。牠們總是把這句格言當成日常生活所不可少的東西。

只要是晴天，一早起，牠們便開始不停地鳴唱。

吱吱喳喳，喞喞啾啾，咕嚕咕嚕，咿咿呀呀，喵嗚喵嗚，嗚嗚哇哇，嘓嘓咯咯⋯⋯牠們鳴唱著，每一聲鳴唱都是一句樂音，珠一般圓，玉一般潤，高昂者有之，低沉者有之，長音者有之，短音者有之，連續者有之，斷續者有之，或強勁，或柔和，或獨唱，或合唱，或齊唱，或輪唱⋯⋯綜合起來，便渾然成為一大合唱。

牠們鳴唱著⋯⋯。

隨著牠們的鳴唱，夜的黑暗漸漸離去，光明的白日隨著太陽的冉冉上升漸漸來臨⋯⋯。

大地的脈搏漸漸動起來了。看，那些花、草、樹木，惺忪的睡眼噙著淚珠，慢慢抬起頭來了。看，那些昆蟲、禽類、獸類，從睡夢中醒轉來，開始叫、走、跑、跳了。看，人們從房子裡走出來了，紛紛出發去做自己應分的工作。⋯⋯

只要是晴天，每天一早，晨鳥便不停地鳴唱著，要唱走黑夜，唱來白天，在窗外，在樹上，在田野⋯⋯。

Singing the Morning Birds

The morning birds are singing, outside the window, on the trees, on the field…

The morning birds are singing, want to sing the dark to go away, and sing the day to come…

In whole the universe, what the most to obey to "early to sleep and early to awake", may be all the birds except owl. They always serve this motto as a daily work which indispensable with.

Just in fine day, as get up in the early morning, they will start to sing ceaselessly.

Chatter-chatter, squeak and chirp, coo-coo, creak-creak, mew-mew, hoot-hoot, guo-guo… they sing. It's a music each voice they sing, round as pearl, smooth as jade, some are high, some are low, some are long, some are short, some are in succession, some are off and on, may strong, may soft, may solo, may chorus, may sing in unison, may round… is a great chorus while sum up.

They are singing…

Follows their sing, the dark of the night departs slowly, the bright day coming gradually after the sun's rising slowly…

The blood pressure of the earth starts to move. Lo, those flowers, grasses and trees raise their heads with the tears within their eyes with sleepy eyes. Lo, those insects, birds, beasts, awake from the dream, start to cry, walk, run and jump. Lo, human beings walk from their house, start all sorts to go to their work within their duty…

Just in fine day, as get up in the early morning every day, the morning birds are singing, want to sing the dark to go away, and sing the day to come, outside the window, on the trees, on the field…

落地生根

落地生根，落地便生根！

是的，落地便生根！土地是財富之母，所有生命的根本。沒有土地，根著何處？生命如何存在、生長、發榮、成熟、結果？

生命需要新陳代謝。上一代需要扶掖下一代；為了成全下一代，甚至可以犧牲自己，使他們能夠繁衍子孫，繼往開來，生生不息。於是，有了這種感人的現象：落葉更護花。更有一種植物，叫做落地生根，而且確確實實做到：落地便生根。

這種現象，看似平常；但是其中包含了多少愛心，多少犧牲，多少情意！

這是怎樣的一種情操！

確實，個體的歲壽有時而盡，大我的生命則是無限的。與其爭一時，何如爭千秋？與其為個體一時的苟活，何如為大我的長存？眼光放大放遠是很必要的。不要只把眼光放在一點，要放在整個宇宙生命的存亡絕續上。只看自己一時的榮辱虛名小利何用？如果對整個宇宙生命的生生不息無益，那只好罷了。

古人老早說過了：「死有輕於鴻毛，有重於泰山。」這就要看人的自我抉擇了。

The Miracle leaf

Miracle leaf, it grows root immediately while leaf falls down on the ground.

Yes, grows root immediately while leaf falls down on the ground. Ground is the mother of wealth, the root of all life. Where root lands without ground? How life exists, grows, flourishes, ripens, bears?

Life needs metabolism. Last generation needs to foster future generation, even to give up self and help to achieve a desired end to future generation, let them can multiply offspring, to carry on the past and open a way for future, grow and multiply without end. Hence, this kind of touching situation will be appeared: more shield flower while the leaf is fell. And more over, there is a kind of plant, called miracle leaf, and do engage surely in it: grows root while leaf falls on the ground.

It looks like common of this kind of situation; but it includes how much love, give up self, affection!

What a kind of sentiment it is!

Certainly, the year of individual will come to an end, the life of every one is endless. Instead of win temporary, how can we win eternal? Instead of live at the expense of principles or hour for individual, how can we strive for the long life of every one? It's need for enlarge your eyes. Don't only put your eyes on a spot, you ought to lay on the life or death of whole the universe. What use for just look at the temporary honour or disgrace and unwarranted reputation and small interest? It will cast if no benefit to grow and multiply without end of the life of whole the universe.

The ancient once said:" Dead is rather heavier than Tarzan and thinner than wild goose's feather." It's up to you to choose.

土香

　　抓一把土，放近鼻尖，聞一聞，哇，好香！

　　是的。土是香的。它散發出濃濃的香味，到處飄飛。如果有一天，土不香了，那就可悲了。

　　生命是不能離開土的。它是生命之源，之泉。任何生命，都需要土；如果離開土，即使不死亡，也難以維持長久生存。

　　植物，無論是花，是草，是樹木，不管是作物，是果樹，有哪一樣可以不要土？

　　動物，是飛禽也罷，是走獸也罷，是昆蟲也罷，以至水中的魚類，有哪一樣可以不要土？

　　至於自稱「萬物之靈」的人類，又何能例外？又何能不需要土？沒有土能生存下去嗎？

　　不！不可能！無論何時，我們都需要土。沒有土，我們便無以立，無以生，無以長。即使死了，我們還需入土，回歸於土。

　　是的。需要入土，需要回歸於土，無論是動物，是植物，是人，絕無例外！

　　所以，我們要愛護土。土是很香的。它們不時散發出濃濃的香味。它們不時提供生命之源，之泉，滋養我們，讓我們得以立，得以生，得以長；我們怎能不愛護，不回報？

　　如果有一天，土不香了，那就可悲了。

Fragrance of the Soil

Hold a bunch of the soil, put it near nose, smell it, wow, how fragrance it is!

Yes, the soil is fragrant. It scatters thick fragrant, flutters everywhere. It's grief if the soil isn't fragrance one day.

Life can't depart the soil. It's the source and spring of life. Any life does need the soil. If life departs the soil, even don't to be died, it also not to maintain exist for a long time.

Plant, no matter is flower, grass, tree, no matter is crop, fruit, what kind of them can't need the soil? Can we exit without the soil?

Animal, in spite of flying bird, beast, insect, as to fish, what kind of them can't need the soil?

As to human being the so call the intelligent part of the universe, how can we except? How can't we need the soil?

No. It's possible! In any case, we need the soil. Without the soil, we can't stand, can't live, grow. Even we die, we still bury into the soil, back to the soil.

Yes, No matter animal, plant or human, all need to bury into the soil, back to the soil.

So, we must cherish the soil. The soil is very fragrant. They often flutter thick fragrance. They often offer source and spring of life, nurture us, let us to stand, to live, to grow; how can't we cherish the soil, to repay the soil?

It's grief if the soil isn't fragrance one day.

珊瑚世界

清洗著，營養著，雕刻著，珊瑚慢慢形成了，一朵又一朵，一叢又一叢，建構成了一個珊瑚世界。

瑩潔，純美，瑩潔純美得一塵不染，讓人不忍稍有觸碰污染之念。那是海水日夜不停清洗的結果。海水是很有耐心的清洗者，也搓，也揉，輕輕地，一次，一次，又一次，絲毫不累，不厭……。

對珊瑚來說，海水是一個乳汁豐沛的母親。她不斷地以其乳汁餵飼珊瑚，營養珊瑚。珊瑚乃順利地生長，生長成各種樹木、花草，生長成鑽石、珠寶、晶石，生長成諸多建築、屋宇、宮殿、房舍，生長成瑩潔、純美……。

海水又是一名精巧無比的藝術家，以其巧藝，不停地雕著，刻著，聚精會神，孜孜不倦。一刀，一鑿，一刀一鑿都見功夫，都留紋痕；不管線條或圖案，都精緻燦麗。那是一種神雕，舉世難尋，人間所無。

這是一個很特殊的地方，一個世外桃源，一個自然生成的「福地洞天」，是那麼瑩潔純美，瑩潔純美得一塵不染，讓人不忍稍有觸碰污染之念，有如鑽石、珠寶、晶石。魚、蝦、蟹等海中動物是穿梭其間、棲息生活其間的族類，可以想像得到是很欣悅、幸福的，過得逍遙而自在。該是神仙生活吧！

要好好保護它！不要去破壞它！

The World of coral

Washing, nurturing, curving, coral forms slowly, a flower after a flower, a tussock after a tussock, set up a world of coral.

Clean, pure, clean and pure into untainted by even a speck of dust, let all others have not any mind to touch. It's the result of the seawater which washes day after night ceaselessly. The seawater is the washer with great patience, will twist, will rub, gently, first time, next time, and next time again, without any weary, be satisfied…

As to coral, the seawater is a mother rich with milk. She feeds coral with her milk ceaselessly, nurtures coral. Coral then grows smoothly, grows into every kind of tree, flower, grass, grows into diamond, pearl, quartz, grows into many buildings, houses, palaces, cabins, grows into clean and pure…

Seawater is also a great delicate artist, carves and chisels ceaselessly with his cleaver skill, be concentrated on, indefatigably. A knife, a chisel, all appears his skill, all remains his texture; in spite of line or pattern, all is delicate and splendor. It is a carve of highly skilled, difficult to find, out of the world.

It's a special place, a garden of the peaches of immortality, a "fu di tong tain", thus clean, pure, clean and pure into untainted by even a speck of dust, let all others have not any mind to touch, like diamond, pearl, quartz. The clan which perches and shuttles among them just as the animals of fish, shrimp and crab can visualize, joyful and happy, live carefree and enjoying themselves. Live with a fairy live!

We ought to protect it, don't to destroy it!

黃槐

　　一棵棵黃槐在校園裡站立著，成排成列，以其肢體站成一個個美的焦點，一片綠的風景；不論直視、橫看或側覽，都那麼美，那麼綠！

　　微風輕輕吹拂而過，成排成列的黃槐便跟著伸展開肢體。

　　好美的線條！好柔的肢體！

　　彷彿一棵棵黃槐都異口同聲地說：

　　「伸展開來！伸展開身體來！……啊，好久沒有伸展開身體來了。好久沒伸展開身體來，各個關節都要生鏽了；一旦伸展開身體來，哇，多舒適！多輕快！」

　　是在做體操吧！一、二、三、四……啊，這是體側舉。這是體側轉。這是俯背運動。這是四肢運動。這是腰部運動。……

　　是在跳舞吧！這是巴蕾。這是勃魯斯。這是探戈。這是恰恰。這是扭扭。這是古典舞。這是民俗舞。這是山地舞。

　　啊，手舉起來了，手往下擺了，手橫張了，單手的，雙手的，配合著音樂的節奏，身體和腳的挪動……。

　　總覺得它們在伸展著肢體，要成長起來，長高，長大，就像校園裡的學生，也要成長起來，長高，長大；事實上也是的：它們和他們都成長起來，長高，長大……。

The Sunshine Tree

There stand a sunshine tree and a sunshine tree in the campus, in rows and in ranks, stand into beautiful focal point with their bodies, a piece of green landscape; all are so beauty, all are so green no matter from what angle to look of them.

Breeze passes by and touches tenderly, sunshine trees stretch their bodies following.

How beautiful the line! How soft the limb!

It seems sunshine tree says one by one with one voice:

"Extend! Extend your body!… Oh, it's how long haven't extended your body. All joints are dust while haven't extended the body for a long time; extend the body in a short time, wow, how comfortable it is! How relaxed it is!"

May the gymnastics! One, two, three, four… oh, it's dumbbell. It's body turning. It's back bend over. It's the exercise of four limbs. It's the exercise of waist.…

May the dance! It's ballet. It's blues. It's tango. It's cha-cha. It's twist. It's classic dance. It's folk dance. It's aboriginal dance.

Oh, hands raise, hands downward, hands stretch, single hand, both hands, match with rhythm of the music, the move of body and feet…

Feeling often that they stretch their bodies and feet, want to grow, grow high, adult, just like the students in the campus, also want to grow high, adult; in fact, they grow match with them, grow into high, adult…

番麥

又到番麥收穫的時候。啊，多令人喜愛的番麥！

一穗穗番麥，被從株梗上摘了下來，堆成一堆堆，然後裝袋，運走……。

開始的時候，先將地整出一壟壟來，把番麥種子播下，覆以鬆土；經過泥土中水分和溫熱的催化作用，番麥發芽了。接著，予以適時的灌水和施肥，番麥便慢慢長高長大，由兩片小小的嫩葉開始，慢慢長出株梗，長出劍狀綠葉，等長到一人高左右，像一片高粱，一片蔗海，便開始結穗。果穗結在長葉的地方，外面有自己長的長鬚和葉莢包裹保護著，慢慢長飽長熟……。

然後，番麥的香味便開始隨風飄送了；由番麥田飄起，飄到農家，飄到市場，又飄到各處人家；不管是生的混有泥土味的香味，是煮熟了的和蒸汽直冒的香味，同樣引人垂涎。好喜愛吸聞！用力地吸氣，深深地吸氣，吸進鄉土，吸進番麥的新鮮和香甜，哇！好香！好舒適！

當煮熟的番麥果穗被剝開葉莢，一股濃濃的喜悅便從心底直衝而出。除了和蒸汽同時冒出的番麥香味而外，那一顆顆果穗上黃澄澄的果粒，如金珠，賽寶玉，盈滿而飽熟，在「炙手可熱」之際，邊吹氣邊趁熱吃，吃得津津有味，齒頰留香。是怎樣一種至高無尚的享受！

好喜愛番麥。它的株梗、劍狀綠葉和果穗，就在眼前，尤其是果穗，更引人無限的遐思……。

The Corn

It's the time of reaping the corn again. Oh, how lovely the corn!

An ear after an ear of corn plucked from the stem, pile into a pile and a pile, then load into the bag, transport…

In the very beginning, soil preparation into a ridge and a ridge in advance, sow the seed of corn, cover the loose soil; the seed will send off bud after the germination of the moisture and warmth of the soil. And to watering and fertile in time, the corn will grow high and adult slowly, grows stem from two tender shoots, grows into sword-like green leaf, and bear ear while it's tall as a man, like a piece of sorghum, like a piece of cane sugar sea. Ear bears on the place which grows leaf, parcels and safeguards with long tassel and blade outside, grows into full and mature…

Then fragrance of corn will start to waft follows the wind, wafts from corn field, to peasant family, to market, once more wafts to families everywhere; no matter the uncooked fragrance mingle with soil, or the fragrance which cooked and steam send out ceaseless, slave everyone as the same. How like to inhale it! Inhale expertly self, inhale deeply, inhale native land, inhale the fresh and fragrance, wow, how fragrance it is! How comfortable it is!

A band of thick joy will push from the bottom of the heart while the blade of the ear of corn is peeled. Besides fragrance send out with steam the same time, the yellow grain one after another juts like golden pearl, gem, full and mature, at the time of "burning to the touch", we take advantage of steam to eat, to eat with appetite and relish, fragrance remain in mouth still. What a kind of highest enjoyment!

I like corn. The stem, blade green leaf and ear appears before my eyes, especial the ear, let me lost in reverie…

茉莉花

好一朵美麗的茉莉花！

好一朵美麗的茉莉花！

芬芳美麗滿枝椏，

又白又香人人誇！

是誰？是誰唱的？多好聽的歌！

別以為茉莉花，花朵小小的，僻處一隅，沒什麼可取的，其實不然，她

天生麗質，

冰清玉潔，

香氣撲鼻，

潔白異常，

純美異常！

絕不渺小，一朵朵是一個個紮實的自我，一個個大千世界，一顆顆珍奇寶物！

絕不卑下，誰都不能看輕她！

光風霽月。

胸懷坦蕩。

她可以睥睨群花，雖然她不願意。

雖然她不願意，她可以和獅子的腳爪比銳利，可以和老虎的利牙較高低，可以和凱撒大帝爭勝負，可以和西施賽美麗……。

啊，茉莉花呀茉莉花！

The Jasmine

What a beautiful jasmine flower
What a beautiful jasmine flower
Sweet-smelling, beautiful, stems full of buds
Fragrance and white, everyone praises
Who? Who sings? What a fine song pleasant to hear!
Don't deem the jasmine is so small, remotes in a corner, it's nothing matters to take a look at, in fact, it's not the case, she is
A born beauty
Pure like jade and clear like ice
Sweet smell assails the nostrils
Pure white extremely
Pure beauty extremely
Not insignificant absolutely, one after one is one and one of sturdy self, one after one of Buddhist cosmology, one after one of precious treasure!
Not despicable absolutely, no one can despise her!
It's light breeze and clear moon.
It's broad and candid.
She can despise all the flowers though she may not desire.
Though she may not desire, she can compare to the sharp of lion's paw, and compare to the sharp teeth of tiger, contend for Caesar, contest the beauty to Hsi Shih…
Oh, jasmine, oh, jasmine!

繁花

　　繁花盛開著，爭豔著，在各處……。

　　在花園裡，有繁花盛開著。看！杜鵑和蘭花爭豔，一丈紅和太陽花比紅，木蘭和桂花競香，梅花和水仙較潔……。其實，何止於此？還有其他許多許多的花呢！它們好像唯恐出力不夠，無法把世界裝飾得夠美，會有深深愧疚；於是，傾出全力，用盡心思，使出渾身解數，競相表現，呼喝之聲，彷彿清晰可聞，一朵比一朵大，一朵比一朵盛，一朵比一朵香，一朵比一朵紅，一朵比一朵豔，集朵成串，集串成叢，朵朵串串叢叢，花枝招展著，繁美紛呈著，美不勝收……。

　　在田野裡，有繁花盛開著，爭豔著。那是稻禾。那是香蕉。那是玉米。那是蓮霧。那是甘蔗。……各種各樣的植物，競相成長、繁盛、壯大、成熟，彷彿不這樣就不夠盡力。那就是一朵朵花，一串串花，一叢叢花，繁花，繁花！

　　同樣地，在人世間，也有繁花盛開著，爭豔著。看！那一棟棟大樓，不斷地蔓延著，生長著，越來越多，越來越大，越來越高。看！各種發明，越來越多，越來越好越方便。……那是人們的智慧之繁花盛開、爭豔的結果。當然，人們的臉上也有繁花盛開、爭豔了……。

　　我要更加努力，獻上我的一份力量，一朵花，讓繁花更繁更盛更美！

Multiplex flowers

Everywhere, there are multiplex flowers full open, contend for beauty...

There are multiplex flowers full open in the garden. Lo! Azalea and orchid contend for beauty, althaea and sunflower compare red, lily magnolia and sweet osmanthus race fragrance, plum blossom and narcissus contend purity... In fact, is it far more than this? There are still many and many other flowers! They seem for fear that not do the best, unable to decorate the world beauty enough, will regret deeply; so, exert to the utmost of their power, use all their idea, use all their skills, to show with each other, the sound to shout seems can be heard clearly, one flower is bigger than the other, one flower is greater than the other, one flower is more fragrance than the other, one flower is redder than the other, one flower is brighter than the other, gather flower into string, gather string into tussock, flower and string and tussock, the flowering branches sway, all sorts of beauty appear, nothing more beautiful can be imagined...

There are multiplex flowers full open in the field and contend their beauty. It's the rice. It's the banana. It's the corn. It's the wax apple. It's the sugar cane... Every kind of plant gather to grow, exuberant, strengthen, ripen, as if it's not stretch enough while not do so. It's a flower and a flower, a string of flower and a string of flower, a tussock and a tussock of flower, multiplex flowers, multiplex flowers!

It's the same, there are also multiplex flowers and contend their beauty all over the world. Lo! A block and a block of big building creep, grow, more and more it increases in number, bigger and bigger they are, higher and higher they are. Lo! Every kind of invention is more and more in number, more and more in good, more and more in invention... It's the result of multiplex flower of people's wisdom open and contend for beauty. Of course, multiplex flower is also open on the face of the people...

I will more strive, and offer my strength and flower, to make the flower more numerous and more thriving and more beauty!

蘭花

　　你喜歡觀賞葉子，還是喜歡觀賞花朵？就任由你選吧！蘭花，就有那麼好的能耐，任人喜歡觀賞葉子還是花朵，它們都能任人精挑細選，各取所需，它們都能盡出渾身解數，大顯其身手，大展其才華。

　　是孤芳自賞也罷！是大家共賞也罷！

　　多少種葉子，

　　多少種花朵，

　　紛呈著。

　　多少種姿態，

　　多少種顏色，

　　紛呈著。

　　在山中，在田野，在森林，它們自由自在地生長，繁榮，開花：有些被人們遷移了，遷移到了花園裡，遷移到了人家的大客廳中，它們照樣自由自在地生長，繁榮，開花，絲毫不受影響。所以，有多少人唱著：

　　我從山中來，

　　帶來蘭花草……

　　你喜歡觀賞葉子，還是喜歡觀賞花朵？那都是絨質的，綢質的，多麼柔和，多麼美好！

　　而且，也喜歡嗅聞它們的芳香吧！

The Orchid

Do you like to appreciate the leaf or the flower? It up to you as you pleased. The orchid has the talent to let people to appreciate. They all promised to let people to handpick, take what they want, they all promised to let people to do what they can, to show what they're all about, to show their talent.

May be self-appreciate own beauty and fragrance! May be appreciated by all!

As many as the leaves,
As many as the flowers,
Come thick and fast.
As many as the postures,
As many as the colours,
Come thick and fast.

In the mountain, in the country field, in the forest, they grow leisurely and carefree, flourishing, bloom: some moved by people to plant in the garden, to the parlour, they still grow and bloom leisurely and carefree, not have any influence on them. So, as many as the people to sing:

I come from the mountain,
Carry the orchid…

Do you like to appreciate the leaf or the flower? They all are flannel-like, silk-like, how soft and how fine they are!

And, you may love to smell the sweet-scented!

勿忘我

　　每個有愛情的人，他的血液中恆流著一朵朵盛綻的紅玫瑰，眼眸恆見一朵朵藍色的勿忘我，翻湧著一河多腦河水，緊緊牽繫著一則傳奇故事……。

　　「勿忘我！」

　　這是誰人的呼喚？這是誰人的衷曲？那麼急切，那麼深含殷殷祈望和無限情愛，那麼深深感動人心肺腑！

　　是從哪裡來的？

　　是從那有愛情的人的藍色眼眸深處傳來的；是從那多腦河水深處傳來的；是從那則藍色傳奇故事深處傳來的。

　　「勿忘我！」

　　冒著生命的危險去摘取一朵藍花，在失足跌入急流已然沒有生還希望的時候，呼喚出這一句話，代表著的是什麼？尤其是，終於抵不住急流的大力，即將遭到滅頂，呼喚出這一句話，代表著的是什麼？

　　不必去問騎士魯德爾夫和他的愛侶蓓兒達了。

　　什麼山盟海誓都不能和這故事，這句話相比。

　　感人呀感人！

　　愛情就是這麼感人！

　　啊，就讓那一朵朵藍色的勿忘我綻放在有愛情的人的眼眸深處吧！就讓多腦河的藍色河水繼續汹湧在那一刻傳奇故事深處吧！

Forget-me-not

Everyone who has the love within always flows a flower and a flower of full blossoming red rose in his blood, a flower and a flower of blue for-got-me-not, surging a river water of Danube, hauls tightly a legendary story...

"Forget- me- not!"

Whose calling is it? Whose aspirations is it? Thus pressing, thus full with earning wish deeply and love limitless, thus touch to others deeply!

Where is it come from?

It's transmitted from the depth of blue eyes of the lover; it's transmitted from the depth of Danube; it's transmitted from the depth of the blue romance .

"Forget-me-not!"

To pluck a blue flower with braves the danger of life, calls this word while falling down in the rushing currents, what does it mean? Especially, he can't resist the big power of the currents and will be drowned, calls this word, what does it mean?

Don't need to ask Rodolph and his lover Bertha .

What pledge of faithfulness and love can compare with this romance and this word?

Touchable, oh, touchable!

Love is thus touchable!

Oh, let a blue forget-me- not open in the depth of the lover's eyes! Let the water of Danube surges in the moment of the depth of the romance successively!

仙草

「天氣這麼熱，來一碗仙草冰，該有多好呀！」

「是呀！那再好不過了！⋯⋯哇，那邊就有嘛，你看！路那邊⋯⋯。」

「好！我們去吃去！」

「喂！仙草是怎麼做的？長得怎樣？你知道嗎？」

「不知道。」

「我們問老闆吧！」

「仙草呀！它們又叫仙草舅、涼粉草、仙人草、仙草凍等，山野路旁到處都有，是一年生草本，全體被有分節的毛，莖方形，帶紅褐色，葉卵形至橢圓形，邊緣有鋸齒，上表面光滑或僅在中肋上具有少許毛，下表面散生毛茸，秋冬開花，花序頂生或腋生，花萼鐘形，二唇，上唇較長，花冠管狀，淡紫色，雄蕊四枚，二長二短，花柱扁平，柱頭二分叉⋯⋯這些說明其實你們也不懂啦，哪，這就是啦，你們看就知道。」

「哇！這麼不起眼呀！」

「別小看它們！把它們的莖葉取來熬汁，加點粉漿及粳油，冷卻後就變成黑紫色洋菜狀物，切成小塊，加入糖水和刨冰或削冰，就是你們現在吃的這些夏日清涼解渴聖品了。不但這樣，仙草還可以降低血壓，治療淋病及腎臟病呢！」

「哇！真奇妙呀！」

The Mesona

"It's so hot, may we have a cup of mesona ice, how good it is!"

"Yes! It could be better!… Wow, it's there, lo! That way beside the road…"

"Well! Let's go!"

"Wei! How to produce mesona ice? What is the image? Do you know?"

"I don't know!"

"May we ask the shopkeeper!"

"As to mesona! They are also called sian uncle, leung fun cho, fairy grass, sian jelly etc, spread everywhere in mountainous area and beside the road, are annuals, they all cape with hairs divide into knot on stem, red brown in colour, the leaves are oval to ellipse, there are sawtooth in the edge, there are smooth or some hairs on the half of the upper face, and there are hairs spread scatter on below face, blossom in summer and winter, florescence grows on top or armpit, clock shape in calyx, two flower lips, it's longer in upper lip, tube shape in corolla, light purple, four pieces of pistil, two long, two short, style flat and plane, two divides in the head… In fact, these explanations you may not know, well, this is it, you may know as you see."

"Wow, so unconspicuous!"

"Not look down upon them! Take their stem and leaves to stew juice, add some starch and stalk oil, they will become black and purple of agar – like things, cut them into block, add sugar water and ice, frappe, they are the sainthood to cool and quench you in summer and you eat now. Not only thus, mesona can low down blood pressure, heal gonorrhea and chronic kidney disease!"

"Wow, how wonderful!"

彩葉草

　　每次看見彩葉草，每次想起彩葉草，在我眼中，在我心裡，便紛呈出許多美姿，許多顏彩：棕、黃、綠、藍、紅、橙、紫、栗……。

　　彩葉草，彩葉草，啊，多少美姿紛呈，多少顏彩紛呈的彩葉草！

　　紛呈呀紛呈，彩葉草紛呈出展綻的焰火，彩繪著多彩多姿，圖案是那麼和諧，線條是那麼柔美，加上繽紛的顏彩，展現出豐富的內容：節慶、自由、和平、安適、滿足、歡笑、悅樂……。

　　紛呈呀紛呈，彩葉草紛呈出一幕幕舞蹈來。那是山地慶祝豐年的舞蹈吧！那是夏威夷的草裙舞！那是我國最正統的民族舞蹈吧！在微風中，在明亮的陽光下，舞者穿著燦然的服飾，展出優美的舞姿，款款而舞，每一動作都應和著音樂的節奏，繫著萬人之眼，萬人之心……。

　　紛呈呀紛呈，彩葉草紛呈出傍晚時分西方天邊塗滿繽紛顏彩的晚霞，晚秋時節楓樹上滿樹紅葉……。

　　紛呈呀紛呈，彩葉草紛呈出美、詩，多彩多姿……。

　　紛呈呀紛呈，

　　以有鋸齒葉緣的彩葉，

　　以由許多藍色小花組成的穗狀花序，

　　以全生命，全心意……。

　　彩葉草，紛呈吧！紛呈出那些美姿，那些顏彩……。

The Coleus

Every time when I meet coleus, every time I think of coleus, there were come thick and fast many good looks and many colours: brown, yellow, green, blue, red, orange, purple, maroon, in my eyes, in my mind…

Coleus, oh, coleus, how many good looks come thick and fast, the coleus which many colours come thick and fast!

Comes thick and fast oh, comes thick and fast, coleus comes thick and fast the fireworks, paints of striking colours, pattern is so harmonious, the line is so soft, increases the colour is in riotous profusion, appears the profusion content: festival, freedom, peace, quiet and comfortable, satisfied, laugh heartily, happy…

Comes thick and fast oh, comes thick and fast, coleus comes thick and fast a stage and a stage of dance. May it be the dance hilly country for celebrating the bumper year! May it be the hula of Hawaii! May it be the folk dance the most formal dance of our country! In the breeze, under the bright sunshine, the dancer in elegant attire, shows fine dance posture and movements, dancing with loving, every movement deals with the rhythm of the music, ties ten thousand of eyes, ten thousand of hearts…

Comes thick and fast oh, comes thick and fast, coleus comes thick and fast the colourful afterglow smears on the western sky at dusk, the red leaves full on the maple tree in the late autumn…

Comes thick and fast oh, comes thick and fast, coleus comes thick and fast the beauty, poem, many good looks…

Comes thick and fast,
With colour sawtooth in the edge of the leaves
With many blue small spikes composed by many small flowers
With whole life, with whole mind…

Comes thick and fast oh, comes thick and fast, comes thick and fast those good looks, those colours…

鳳仙花

　　在那些年代裡，把鳳仙花採來，搗碎，用布包裹在指甲上，染紅指甲，是少女們一種殷切的期望，一種流行於當時的習俗。

　　鳳仙花，多像一隻飛鳥，意欲飛起；

　　而其殷紅，正是少女的丹心。

　　這些或許是許多人很關心很感興趣的；我最關心最感興趣的卻是果實成熟後，不管有沒有人碰，總會自然裂開，彈出種子，彷彿在說：

　　「但願有一天，被冤枉的事，會水落石出！」

　　「清清白白，絕無隱瞞。我隨時都願接受探查。」

　　世間到處都可能有陰暗的一面；但是太陽一到，光明便顯現了。

　　天空一片蔚藍，是多麼美好！但總會有被雲翳遮蔽的時候；只要風一來，雲翳被吹散，總會現出蔚藍的本來面目。

　　即使奧林帕斯宮殿中那名仙女都有可能被冤枉，何況凡間？但是濁者自濁，清者自清，任何沉冤，任何不白，終有水落石出的時候。

　　「但願有一天，被冤枉的事，會水落石出！」

　　「清清白白，絕無隱瞞。我隨時都願接受探查。」

　　坦誠，以肝膽與人相照，絕不怕被冤，裂開蒴果，彈出種子，敞開胸懷，禁受任何探查考驗吧！

The Garden Balsam

In those ages, takes the garden balsam, smashes them into pieces, parcels in with nail, dyes nail into red, is the urgent yearn for girl, a custom prevailing at that time.

Garden balsam, how like it is a flying bird, intend to fly;

And its red, is just the royal heart of the girl.

Those may be great minded and interested by many people; however, I mind and interested the most is when the fruit ripe, no matter it's touched or not, it always will burst naturally and spring the seed, as if it says:

"Wishing the injustice the time will come to reveal the whole truth."

"Be an honorable person doing honorable things, not keep back the truth at all. I'll like to be searched for at any time."

There are gloomy side everywhere in this mortal world; but the sun comes, bright will appear.

How fine is the blue sky! But there was the time often covered by the cloud; just the wind is here, the cloud will be get loose by the wind, it always appears the true feature.

Even the maiden in palace of Olympic may be treated unjustly, let along this mortal world? However, the wise man knows he knows nothing, the fool thinks he knows all, any thing be unjustly will be the time comes to reveal the whole truth.

"Wishing the injustice the time will come to reveal the whole truth."

"Be an honorable person doing honorable things, not keep back the truth at all. I'll like to be searched for at any time."

Frank, sworn brothers, never be afraid of be unjustly, burst out capsule, spring the seed, wide open breast, to accept any search and test!

太陽花

　　是誰？是誰有如此其大的力量，把太陽猛力抓了下來，放在地上？

　　是的，太陽是被抓了下來，放在地上了，而且，一放，便分化成了一個個小太陽，綻放盛放在地上！

　　是的，那確實是地上的太陽！——不是地上的太陽是什麼？

　　一朵朵，圓圓的；

　　一瓣瓣紅色線狀花瓣

　　是一條條光芒，

　　四散飛射，

　　照耀得

　　到處光明，燦亮。

　　是的，那確實是地上的太陽！——不是地上的太陽是什麼？

　　在大地上，

　　一個個小太陽，

　　這裡那裡地

　　綻放出無限光芒，

　　綻放出一個個小小的自我……。

　　祈願太陽花，綻放在大地，盛放在大地，給大地帶來光明！

　　——不只綻放，而且盛放，直到永遠！

The Portulaca grandiflora

It's who? It's who possess such a great power catches down the sun vigorously, puts on the earth?

Yes, the sun is caught down, put on the earth, and immediately divided into a sun after a sun, blossomed fully on the earth.

Yes, it's surely the sun of the earth! –what is it if it's not the sun of the earth?

A flower after a flower, round and round;

A piece and a piece of red line-like petal

Are a line and a line of ray,

Sparkle out,

Illuminate into bright and brilliance

Everywhere

Yes, it's surely the sun of the earth! –what is it if it's not the sun of the earth?

On the earth

The little sun one after another

Blossoming

Limitless ray

Either and thither,

Blossoming one by one of little self...

Wishing portulaca grandiflora blossom on the earth, on the earth fully, bring brilliance to the earth!

–Not only blossom, but also blossom fully, forever!

葡萄

　　一串串葡萄垂掛著，顆粒纍纍，在枝葉間，在支架上……。

　　在枝葉間，在支架上，垂掛著，一串串：紫葡萄、綠葡萄、白葡萄……。

　　垂掛著，從小小的顆粒開始，從瘦瘦的身段開始，從皺皺的表皮開始，從酸酸的味道開始，從極輕極輕開始，從生澀生澀開始，漸次生長，越生長顆粒越大，越生長越渾圓，越生長果肉越飽滿，越生長味道越甜蜜，越生長越有重量，越生長越成熟……。

　　啊，終於成熟了！

　　一串串，一顆顆，甜而多汁，入口即化，不需費什麼勁去咬嚼，是大自然靈氣的集合，天真地秀、日月光華的凝聚，是造物的巧手親自調理精製而成的。那會是多麼神奇的真滋味！

　　一串串，一顆顆，晶質的，微微透出晶光。是柑橘汁？是檸檬露？是草莓霜？是番茄醬？是杏仁豆腐？……

　　哇！好美呀！一串串，一顆顆，是白玉？是翡翠？是晶石？是翠玉？是如意？是寶石？是真珠？……

　　令人想起，佳人襟上、胸前、臂間、手腕、手指所戴的寶玉、真珠、戒指、手鐲……。

　　一串串葡萄垂掛著，顆粒纍纍……啊，那是一串串葡萄珠串！

The Grape

There are cluster after cluster of grapes hang down from the branches, from the frameworks, a grain after a grain…

From the branches, from the frameworks, hang down, a cluster and cluster, the purple grape, the green grape, the white grape…

Hang down, begins from the little grain, begins from the thin and small body, from the crape skin, from the sour, from the thinnest and thinnest, from unripe, grows slowly, bigger and bigger while growing, rounder and rounder while growing, plumper and plumper while growing, sweeter and sweeter while growing, more and more in weight while growing, more and more mature while growing…

Oh, it's mature at last!

A cluster after a cluster, a grain after a grain, the grape is sweet and juicy, just melt in the mouth, don't need to bite laborously, it's the collection of nature sovereign remedy, the collection of grandeur of the universe, is refined intensively by Creator himself. How wonderful is the true taste!

A cluster after a cluster, a grain after a grain, it's crystal, shines little crystalline light. Is it the juice of orange? Is it the dew of lemon? Is it the frost of strawberry? Is it the tomato sauce? Annin tofu?…

Wow! How great the cluster and grain! Is it the white jade? Is it the jadeite? Is it the crystal? Is it the green jade? Is it the ruyi? Is it the gem or the pearl?…

It let me think of the gem, pearl, ring, bracelet which wears on beautiful woman's front of a garment, breast, arm, trick and finger…

There are cluster after cluster of grape hang down, a grain after a grain… oh, it's a cluster after a cluster of pearl of the grape!

土豆

說土豆「向下扎根，向上開花」，是通的；說土豆「向下扎根，向上結果」，則是笑話。綜合起來，說土豆「向下扎根，向上開花，向下結果」，是最適切了。

一般稱它為花生，很符合實際；因為它確實先開花後結果！但是我們大都叫它土豆，更符合實際；原因無他，它在長出地面的莖上開花，然後埋進地下土裡結「豆」。

兩種名稱比較起來，我還是比較喜歡土豆這個名稱。

為什麼不稱它為土豆呢？該這樣稱呼才對呀！為什麼不喜歡這個名稱呢？該喜歡這個稱呼才對呀！

土豆，多麼土的名稱，多麼好的豆子呀！不管是湯煮，是剝了殼或不剝殼炒，同樣是香噴噴的，尤其是炒的，除了香而外，更加上脆，真是香脆可口！至於它的營養，那更不用說了。這樣的東西，誰會不喜歡？身體得助益了，吃過後又能齒頰留香，加上其植株的靈巧姣好，更叫人愛不忍釋了。

一顆顆小小的豆子，一莢莢小小的豆子，一串串小小的豆子，埋在地下，靜靜地，默默地，不求人知，不去炫耀，不去張揚，獨樂自處，自我藏拙，自我滿足，自我生長；當長大成熟，被人從土裡挖起來吃食，才發揮自己的特長，以其營養和香脆貢獻出自己的智慧和力量。這是多麼美好的德行呀！

土豆，我不能不喜歡！

The groundnut

We can say groundnut "takes root on the earth, and blossoms upward"; but it's joke to say groundnut "takes root on earth, and fruits upward". Summarily, to say "takes root on the earth, blossoms upward, and fruits on the earth." is the most suitable.

Name it generally as groundnut is tally with facts; because it's sure that it blossoms in front of and fruits thereafter! But we all call it groundnut is the most suitable; no other cause, it blossoms on the stem which grows on the ground, and then fruits "bean" which bury in the ground.

I still more like to call the name groundnut compares with these two names.

Why don't we call it groundnut? It's right for us ought to call it this name! Why don't we like this name? It's right for us ought to call it this name!

Groundnut, how original the name, how good is the bean! In spite of soup-boiling, parch it with exploiting the shell, it's rich in fragrance the same, especially exploiting, except fragrance, adds of fragile, it's fragrant and fragile surely! As to nutrition, it's no need to say. Whoever will dislike this kind of thing? It helps to body, and will remain fragrance after have it, adds to the pretty and good feature, it'll more love can't let go.

A grain after a grain of the small bean, a pod after a pod of the small bean, a string after a string of the small bean, bury in the ground, silently, quietly, not to seek for known, not to show off, not to make publicly known, happy self and lives self, hides self, satisfies self, grows self; when it grown, and dug out by people to eat, it just brings into play its strong point, offers its wit and power with its nutrition and fragile. How fine is its ethics!

Groundnut, I can't help to like it!

尋夢草

　　酢醬草是鄉下田野間常見的一種匍匐性野草花，有一則關於它們的傳說，在田野間流傳著：

　　酢醬草的葉子是由三枚小葉合成的。在這些葉子間，偶然會有一種變種的葉子，是由四枚小葉合成的。這就叫做幸運草。尋找到幸運草的人，一定可以得到某種幸運。

　　好美的傳說！小孩子們總給編織成很美的夢，並到酢醬草叢裡去尋尋覓覓，尋覓得滿身是汗，想尋覓出一棵幸運草，去實現他們的夢。

　　何止小孩子呢？其他的人何獨不然？生而為人，不分男女老幼，人人有夢。為了實現這個夢，人人尋覓，不怕風吹雨打，冬冷夏熱，不管何時何地，都在尋覓。

　　沒有人不希望尋找到幸運草。沒有人不希望美夢成真。能尋找到幸運草多好！美夢能成真多好！即使只有一點點可能性，即使只是一則傳說，還是這麼希望。

　　日復一日，年復一年，人們不斷地尋覓著，甚至上窮碧落下黃泉。不為什麼，他們是在尋找幸運，追尋夢。

　　命運掌握在自己的手中。豐收是付出許多血汗得來的。幸運躲在最隱密的地方，不輕易示人。只有努力尋找的人，他才會出面，才會被尋找到。等待只有落空；追尋便能獲得。

　　「我找到了。」這是很令人驚喜的話。人人切望有一天能這樣喊叫出來。但願人人都有這樣喊叫出來的一天！

The Clover Looking for Dream

Oxalis is a kind of creeping wild grass often find on country field. There is the hearsay about them spreads in the field:

The leaf of oxalis is composed by three slight leaves. Among these leaves, there is a kind of leaf occasionally composed by the variety, it's composed by four slight leaves. It's called lucky clover. The person who has looked out lucky clover will certainly obtain some lucky.

How wonderful the hearsay! The children always want to weave them into dream, and looking for them among the jungle of oxalis, looking to be sweat full of body, wishing to look out a lucky clover, to let their dream to come true.

By no means limited to the children? Why not the others? Born to be a human being, no matter male or female, old or young, everyone has a dream. In order to make the dream come to true, everyone is looking for, no afraid of wind and rain, winter cold and summer hot, in spite of wherever and whenever, all are looking for.

No one unwished-for find the lucky clover. No one unwished-for let his beautiful dream to be come true. How great when find out lucky clover! How great when beautiful dream come true! Even just a bit of possibility, even it just the hearsay, still wish as thus.

A day after a day, a year after a year, people look for successively, even look for into heaven and nether world. No for what purpose, they are looking for lucky, looking for dream.

Destiny is on own hands. Offer much blood and sweat to obtain harvest. Lucky takes shelters in the most secret place, can not appear casually. Only the person who strives to look for it, he may appear to be found. Just come to naught if waiting; looking for it will obtain.

" I find out!" This is the word surprised to everyone. Everyone yearn for to call out one day. Wishing everyone will call as thus one day!

蓄電池

作家應該是蓄電池。

對於蓄電池不應該只看它的外表。它的外表，立體，或方，或圓，硬硬的，呆板，漆黑，粗糙，給人以骯髒的感覺，甚至使人心生厭惡。它的內在則不如此，雖然只有一些鉛板和硫酸稀釋溶液，卻能儲蓄著電：電燈需電時，一接通便能大放光明；馬達需電時，一接通便能發動；如果電少了，只要有鋅板和硫酸稀釋溶液，便可再充電，再儲蓄電；電充夠了，儲蓄夠了，再拿來使用，發揮它的功能……如此循環不已。

有些讀者在和作家見面以前，很崇拜他，但是和他見了面以後便冷了；因為見他相貌不過爾爾呀！這樣的讀者，便是以外表取人的，分明庸俗不堪。他們是以看電影明星或歌星的態度來看作家的。其實，作家是不能用這種態度來看的。電影明星或歌星往往是以外表取勝的，常常要作秀，要流行。一個作家如果和電影明星或歌星一樣，一天到晚穿得花紅柳綠，到處作秀、開會、座談，跟著人家流行，他便該被除籍了。作家要是蓄電池，外表不一定美麗，內在則需美麗，尤其心靈應該多儲蓄，以便有能力點亮蠟燭，燭照世人，引人出迷津，走向光明。那麼，作家像蓄電池，常充電便很重要了。充了電，儲夠了電，才有能力點亮蠟燭，燭照世人呀！

所以我說：作家應該是蓄電池。

The Storage Battery

Writer ought to be the storage battery.

We ought not to look only the appearance about storage battery. Its appearance is solid, may square or circular, hard, idiot, blackened, rough, offers the feeling of dirty, even arose boring. On the contrary, it's not just like that, it can store electricity though it just some stereotype and thin liquid sulphuric acid, yet it can store electricity: the lamp will burning brightly in the sky as if it connect with; the motor will move as if it connect with; when there lack of electricity, just there is stereotype and thin sulphuric acid, it can charge electricity again, store electricity again; and use it when it charged enough electricity, stored enough electricity, plays the role of it… circle ceaselessly.

Some readers worship the writer before they meet him, but faint after met him; because they know him just like this! This kind of reader is judged a person by the appearance, it's too vulgar obviously. In fact, the writer can't know with this manner. The movie star or singer often can win through appearance, often need show, need in fashion. If a writer likes the movie star or singer, wears in bonuses Liulv, shows, attends in meeting, informal discussion in fashion as all others, he ought to be dismiss from this party. A writer must be the storage battery, he is not necessarily be beauty all day long, but he must beauty in internality, particularly there are storage in his mind, in order to kindle the candle to illuminate other people, lead them to guide someone how to get onto the right path, go to bright way. And then, it's very importance for a writer to charge electricity. Charged electricity, stored enough electricity, will enable him to kindle candle, and illuminate other people!

So I say, a writer ought to be the storage battery.

晴朗的夏晨

每到夏日，清晨一起床，看見天氣晴朗，我的心中便充滿喜悅，便情不自禁地在心中歡呼著：

「啊，多麼晴朗的早晨！」

「啊，美好的日子來了！」

是的，在這晴朗的夏晨，我有把握，日子必將美好！

清涼的晨風，正徐徐吹來，吹撫得萬物舒適酣暢，醺然欲醉，吹撫得人輕鬆愉快。

所有的植物都繁發滋長，欣欣向榮。花兒著花紛繁，展現著諸多形貌色彩，吐露出芬香。草木扶疏碧綠，給人以一股新生力量，極大衝勁……。

鳥兒在鳴唱，在奏樂。牠們正揮發其所有的能力，在田野，在林間，在空際。多麼好聽呀！可以悅我耳，可以清我心！

太陽在東方冉冉昇起，閃射出無限光芒，把各處照耀得光明燦亮，使我看了，對這個世界抱持著無限希望，堅信前途必然光明，道路必然寬廣、平坦而長遠，走前去必然美好順遂，不會有任何荊棘、風波或阻難。

一往直前的信心乃在我的心中醞釀成熟。哦，且向前跨步！且向前尋求！且向前抓取！

怎麼可能有什麼不快？在這麼晴朗的夏晨，怎能不抱希望，對這個世界？啊！在這晴朗的夏晨，我已看見，美好的日子來了。

The Sunny Dawn of the Summer

When it's summer, as get up at dawn, knowing it's sunny, my mind will fill with joyousness, and can't help from acclaim:

"Ah, how fine the dawn!"

"Ah, the fine day is coming!"

Yes, in the sunny dawn of the summer, I can affirm, the day must be fine.

The refreshing breeze is blowing gently, caresses all the things into comfortable and delightful, drunken, blowing the person into relaxed with a light heart.

All plants are flourishing and grow. The flowers open numerous and complicated, appear many images and shapes, pour out fragrance. The grasses and trees are green and luxuriant and well-spaced, gift us puff of new power, great impulse…

The birds are singing, playing. They play the role of their ability, on the field, in the forest, on the sky. How fine to hear! It can please my ears, wash my mind.

The sun raising slowly from the east, shines radiance unlimited, brightens all places, let me embrace hope unlimited, and affirm there must be bright in the future, the road must be wide, smooth and long, must be fine and easy and smooth, there won't any thorns, disturbance or obstruct…

The faith to go ahead directly contained and formed in my mind. Oh, to step forward! To search forward! To grasp forward!

How can we unhappy? On this sunny dawn of the summer, how can we not embrace the hope toward this world?

Oh, in this sunny dawn of the summer, I know the fine day is coming.

康乃馨

一朵康乃馨活現在我的眼前，活現在我的心中，輝光閃閃……。

總在五月裡開放，總開放得那麼壯盛，那麼嚴肅，那麼深具意義……。

它，到底是怎麼樣的一種花？

它是一種充滿讚美和感恩的花！

所有的根莖，所有的枝葉，都在收斂，都在凝聚，都在輸送，收斂凝聚一種異樣的光輝，然後輸送給花，給花去開放，去表現，去歡呼……。

那是一種讚美。

那是一種感恩。

那是一種自我期許。

每一瓣花瓣都發出一句句讚美，每一瓣花瓣都寫著一句句感恩，每一瓣花瓣都輝映著一句句自我期許：

──慈暉母愛，永世長存，人間永沐！

──要有母愛，才有大地萬物的發榮滋長！

──母親的恩惠，如山高，如海深，永難報答！

──在母親面前，無論長得多高，無論有多大成就，永遠是小孩，永遠渺小，永遠要感恩！

──努力奮發，以報答親恩！

我希望，我祈求，我手中拿著的康乃馨，永遠是紅色的，不會是白色的。

The Carnation

A carnation appears vividly before my eyes, appears vividly in my heart, with radiance...

It always blossoms in May, always blossoms thus grandeur, thus severe, thus meaningful...

What kind of flower is it?

It's a kind of flower full of praise and be graceful for kindness!

The roots and stems, the branches and leaves, all are draws their horns, all are in coherent sheaves, all are transport, draws their horns and in coherent sheaves into a different radiance, then transports to flowers, let the flowers to blossom, to show, to hail...

It's a praise!

It's a graceful for kindness!

It's a self expectation!

Every petal sends off a praise, every petal writes down a graceful for kindness, every petal shines brilliantly of self expectation:

-Maternal love kindly, long live eternally, bath eternally all over the world!

-It must the maternal love for everything of the earth to thriving and propagate!

-The grace of mother, high like the mountain, deep like the sea, is difficult to repay forever!

-In front of mother, in spite of how tall we grow, how large our achievement, we are children forever, we are insignificant forever, and will graceful for kindness forever!

-We must strive to show great animation, and repay for the grace of mother!

I hope, I pray, the carnation hold in my hand, will be red forever, and never be white.

新頁

不管是自然的律則，還是人為的作用，舊的一定要過去，新的一定要來。

常常我們要翻過舊的一頁，翻開一頁新頁。

翻過舊的一頁，翻開一頁新頁。那是日曆，是書冊，是簿本，是雜誌，是報紙⋯⋯。翻過舊的一頁，翻開一頁新頁，所翻的是一日日，一月月，一年年。所翻的是世事，是歷史。

新頁，好簇新，是一名名小小的嬰孩，紅冬冬的，給人們帶來歡笑和希望，是一棵棵剛發芽的幼苗，將要成長壯大，枝葉茂盛，結實成熟，有豐碩的收穫，是一個未開發的處女地，新發現的礦源，等待開發、耕耘、挖掘，發揮地利，是初升的太陽，會冉冉上升，給人世間帶來無限溫暖和光明⋯⋯。

新頁，和舊的相比，將是更豐富的，更充實的，更精緻的，更繁榮的，更美麗的，更良善的，更開放的，更遼闊的，更恢宏的，更安和的⋯⋯至少至少，這是大家之所至期切望的。

且讓舊的過去，新的來臨！那是一種必然，像一股洶湧的浪潮，要擋也擋不住，要堵也堵不了。

不用憂慮，不必害怕，勇敢地翻過舊的，翻開新的，翻開歷史新頁！

New Page

No matter it's the rule of nature, or it's the function of man-made, the old must be past, the new must be here.

We often turn past the old page, and open a new page.

Turn past the old page, open a new page. That is the calendar, the book, the note book, the paper... Turn past the old, open a new page, all we turn is the day, the month, the year. What we turn are the affairs of the world, the history.

New page, is new, is the baby one and one, all red, brings laugh with joy and hope to people, is the bud just sprout, will be grow and strengthen, luxuriant in the branch, bear fruits and ripen, have rich harvest, is a maiden land undeveloped, a new mineral source, awaits for exploit, cultivate, dig out, play the role of the favourable geographical condition, the sun just raised, will raise slowly, bring to the world warmth and bright limitless...

Compares to the old page, the new page will more abundant, more reinforce, more exquisite, more flourishing, more beauty, better, opener, wider, more magnanimous, more stability... This is all what we hope at least.

May let the old pass, come the new! That's a necessary, like the tide surging, can't stop if you want to stop, can't block if you want to block. Don't worry, don't fear, turn past the old bravely, open the new, open the new page of the history!

牽牛花

伸展，伸展，再伸展，向前方，向四方，向無盡的遠方，伸展開來……。

伸展開來，向前方，向四方，向無盡的遠方，甚至遇到高挺的物體，便攀緣而上，向高處伸展……。

然後，著花了，在那樣的黃昏，春末的黃昏，夏初的黃昏……。

是多麼柔和的黃昏！暖和的微風徐徐而來，夕陽的柔暉遍灑大地，並以其絕藝在西天抹上彩霞……。

就在此刻，牽牛花著花了。

那是造物的無形大彩畫吧！它而且全用的紫色！沒多久，便把一睹牆壁塗得到處是紫色了；沒多久，便把一片綠籬塗得到處是紫色了……。

那是一群紫衣仙女下凡來了吧！一個，一個，又一個，沒多久，便來了好多了，而且迎著暖和的微風，伸展四肢，輕挪蓮步，應和著音樂的節拍，放開胸懷，款款而舞，搖曳生姿……。

那是一支支紫色的長喇叭，在黃昏裡，迎著暖和的微風，吹奏著樂曲。那麼多的長喇叭，昂然挺向天空，是任何樂隊所不能及的。

伸展，伸展，再伸展，伸展開來，是一支造物的無形大彩筆在畫畫也罷，是一群紫衣仙女在跳舞也罷，是一隊樂隊在吹奏長喇叭也罷，總之，伸展開來！

The Morning-glory

Stretch, stretch, stretch again, stretch forward, toward all direction, toward the distance limitless, stretch out…

Stretch out, stretch forward, toward all direction, toward the distance limitless, even climb to the high place when there block by the high and erect thing…

And then, it blossoms, in the dusk, in the dusk of late spring, in the dusk of early summer…

What a soft dusk it is! The warm breeze blows slowly, the soft afterglow full spreads on the earth, and smears rosy glow with his unique art…

The morning-glory is blossoming at this moment.

May it be the great colour paint of invisible of the Creator! And also it's all purple! Just a moment, it smears whole the wall into purple; just a moment, it smears whole the green fence into purple…

May it be a group of purple fairies come from heaven! One after another, and another once again, just a moment, there comes many of them, and face the warm breeze, stretch their four limbs, move their steps lightly, echo to the metre of the music, open their mind, dancing slowly, swinging and swaying of graceful posture…

May it be the purple long trumpet one by one, in the dusk, face to the warm breeze, play the music. So many the trumpet, in a dignified manner toward the sky, no any orchestra can compare.

Stretch, stretch, stretch again, stretch out, may it be a great color brush of invisible by the Creator in painting, may it be a group of purple fairies in dancing, or may it be an orchestra playing the long trumpet, above all, stretch out!

夏的韻味

夏有夏的韻味，和別的季節不同。

夏的韻味是濃烈的。

夏天是豐盛、繁榮、繽紛、豪放、活力充滿的季節。

雲已不再是薄薄的微雲了，通常都是濃濃的一大片烏雲，具有嚇人的嘴臉，一來便把大地籠罩在黑暗之中，並且一高興便下起雨來。那雨可不是毛毛細雨，總是傾盆的滂沱大雨，大得常常打痛萬物的肌膚，伴著轟隆隆的雷聲和金蛇般倏現的閃電，令膽小者被驚嚇得以為世界末日已經降臨。

天晴的時候，烈日當空，火傘高張，燒烤得大地有如在爐火之中。人們總是揮汗如雨，尤其是農人、工人等在烈日下工作的人，不但揮汗如雨，更且在烈日的曝曬之下，受最嚴酷的錘鍊，被烈日的拳頭捶得皮膚一層層脫去，脫去了仍然不住地錘鍊，錘鍊成為赤紅黧黑，光滑得閃發鋼似的微光。

生命更充沛了。活動更熱絡了。冬眠的蟲、蛇、蛙、鼠諸動物早已在春天時甦醒，此時正和其他諸種動物到處爬、走、跑、跳、叫，熱鬧非常。花、草、樹木諸植物發榮滋長，扶疏繁茂，葉子碧綠、釉綠、濃綠，花朵盛放，顏色繽紛，並漸次結果，甚至連無生物也「熱漲冷縮」，一再地膨漲，膨漲，再膨漲……。

夏是豐盛、繁榮、繽紛、豪放、活力充沛的季節。

夏的韻味是濃烈的。

就人來說，這不正是人的盛年？人在盛年，是豐盛、繁榮、繽紛、豪放、活力充沛的，韻味是濃烈的。

願你常時處在盛夏！

The Graceful Manner of Summer

There is the graceful manner of summer, no the same of other seasons. The graceful manner of summer is rich and bright.

Summer is the season of hearty, flourishing, in riotous profusion, unbridled and full of vitality.

Cloud is no more the weak cloud of feeble, is often a stretch black cloud of denseness, has the feature of scare, shrouds whole the world within the darkness as soon as it comes, and rains as it want. The rain is not the drizzle, but often the heavy downpour, often strong to beat all things in the universe into ache, accompany with the booming of thunder and golden snake-like of the lightning, to scare the chicken-hearted to deem it's the befall of the end of the world.

When it's the fine day, the raging sun on the sky, the fire-umbrella wide opened, burning the world as if it's in the stove. All human being often perspiration comes down like raindrops, especially the person working under the sun as the farmer, worker etc., not only perspiration comes down like raindrops, moreover, scorches under the sun, stands the severest temper, tempered by the fist of scorch sun to peel the skin a layer after a layer, tempers still after peeled, tempers into red and black, polishes to shine the steel like tiny light.

Life is more abundant. Activity is more bustling. The hibernate animals as insect, serpent, frog and mouse etc. revive for a long time of the spring, they are climbing, walking, running, jumping, and crying with the other animals, very bustling. The plants as flower, grass and tree are growing and flourishing, luxuriant and well-spaced, bright green, glazy green, rich and bright green the leave, full open the flower, in riotous profusion the colour, fruiting one after another, even inanimate object also "to expand when hot and to shrink when cold", expand again and again, expand, expand again…

Summer is the season of hearty, flourishing, in riotous profusion, unbridled and full of vitality.

The graceful manner of summer is rich and bright.

As to human being, is this not the prime of life? Prime of life is of hearty, flourishing, in riotous profusion, unbridled and full of vitality, the graceful manner of summer is rich and bright.

Wishing you always at the height of the summer!

夏夜的風

　　夏夜的風是最可愛最受歡迎的。白日裡，炎炎夏日，凌虐大地，把萬物給曬得熱得疲憊焦渴不堪，當千眼的夜，在多彩的黃昏前導下，姍姍降臨大地，便有了這麼一陣陣習習晚風，柔和清涼，使萬物如大旱之逢甘霖，滿足了它們所有的千企萬盼。

　　夏夜的風到處遊走著，走過田野，踩過產業道路和田間小徑，穿過諸多作物和果樹，掀起了作物和果樹的一片騷動，款款而語。只為了夏夜的風來臨了，稻子便更成熟了，瓜果便更成熟了，飽滿圓熟的顆粒，正纍纍垂掛著；西瓜、南瓜、小玉、哈密瓜等則躺在地上；圓鼓鼓的，越躺越大，幾欲迸裂，等待收割採擷。

　　眾鳴蟲組成的大樂隊是最起勁了，猛彈猛吹猛奏，嗚嗚哇哇，咿咿呀呀，唧唧啾啾，節奏優美，和諧雅致。如果要說最賣力的，該數吹小喇叭的蟋蟀和吹黑管的螻蛄了。有什麼喜事嗎？只為了夏夜的風來臨了！牠們正以這曲交響樂來迎迓。而且還不僅如此呢！聽，鳴蛙一直鼓掌不停。好大好熱烈的掌聲！看，好心的螢火蟲一直提著燈在照引。怕夏夜的風迷路呀！

　　對於人類，夏夜的風是最公正無私的。它們遊走著，把清涼送給人們。只是鄉野比較歡迎它們，它們來去自如；都市裡則有許多高樓大廈來阻隔它們，它們沒法進去，只好在外面遊走，徒嘆奈何？

The Wind of Summer Night

The wind of summer night is the most lovable and be welcomed. During day time, the raging sun do great damage to the earth, shines all things in the universe that they are exhausted by the hot, when the night of thousand eyes falls slowly on the earth led by the dusk of riotous colour, there is a spell and a spell of dusk wind blow gently, soft and cool, let them obtain as a great rain after a long drought, content all of their wishes.

The wind of summer strolls everywhere, strolls over the field, treads over the industrial road and countryside path, passes through many crops and fruit trees, raises a piece of riot, speeches sincerely. Just for the arriving of the summer wind to befall, rice is more mature, melon and fruit are more mature, grain plump and mature hanging clusters and clusters. Watermelon, pumpkin, chao-yu melon, hami melon etc. lay on the ground, round and round, the larger the longer they lay, almost to be split, waiting to be leaked and plucked.

Numerous singing insects composed an orchestra is the most with zest and vigour, extremely to play, toot, hoot, creak, wow, chirp, twitter, graceful in the rhythm, harmony and elegant. It ought to be the cricket plays with the trumpet and the mole cricket play with the saxophone work hard the most. Is there any happy event? Just for the wind of summer night is befallen! They just welcome it with this symphony. And it is not only thus! May you hear, the frog's call is clapping ceaselessly. How large and how bustle is the clap! Lo, the kind mind firefly takes a lamp to illuminate all the time. For afraid of the summer lost the road!

As to human, the wind of summer is the most equitable. They stroll everywhere, share the cool to everyone. Just the countryside welcomes them more, they free to dealings; there are many big buildings and mansions to bar them to enter in the city, they just stroll outside, what then can I do?

游泳去

「游泳去！」

「好！」

烈日當空，夏日正盛。「好熱！」這話到處可以聽到。是熱呀！好多人前往游泳。游泳正是這季節裡最熱門的事。

其實，游泳不只是浸涼而已，它更有積極的意義。它是一種很好的運動，是廣及全身的。想想，當一個人進入水裡游泳，有哪一部分不浸到水？有哪一部分不在運動？不管是蛙式、蝶式、仰式、自由式，甚至狗爬式，甚至只浸在水裡不動，都能獲得運動的效益，都能嘗到游泳的美味。

水有水性，人有其重量，不懂水性，下水必沉；但是如何使其不但下水不沉，反而浮而能遊？這豈止是口說為憑的事？沒有下過水的游泳教練，說得頭頭是道，下水仍然必沉必溺。所以必需下水，實際去游，去經驗。學什麼東西，實際去做，去經驗，是最重要的工夫。一回生，二回熟，漸漸地便學會了。至於錯誤，那是免不了的，沒什麼好怕。學習本來就是嘗試錯誤的歷程；如果能由錯誤中得到經驗，達到成功，那又何樂不為？

游泳去！夏熱時候，大家是最喜歡去游泳的了。但游泳不只是浸在水裡消暑而已，它更有積極的意義。我們去游泳，是要追求這意義。

Let's go Swimming

"Let's go swimming!"

"Okay!"

Here is the raging sun, the summer is vigorous. "Great hot!" We can hear this word everywhere. It's certain hot! There are many persons go to swimming. Swimming is just the most popular thing in this season.

In fact, swimming isn't just to soak and cool self, it has the positive meaning. It's a good exercise, is extensive to whole body. May you think, when a person enters the water to swim, is there which part of the body not soak to the water? Is there which part of the body is not in exercise? No matter breaststroke, butterfly stroke, backstroke, freestyle swimming, even dog paddle, even only soak within the water without move, will obtain benefit of the exercise, will taste the flavour of the swimming.

There is the characteristics of the current, and there is the weight of the person, if one ignores of the characteristics, he will be sunk; how to free from sinking into the water only, on the contrary to float on the water to swim? Is it only relies on the matter of verbal expressions? The swim coach instructor explains clear and convincing, he'll surely sink and dead still while he enters the water. So one must enter the water to swim, to experience. To do reality and experience is the most important work while you learn anything. Difficult at first but easy later on, then you'll do it well slowly. As to mistake, it can't escape, no any fear of. Learning originally is the course of trying the mistake; what's the sense of not doing it while we can obtain experience from mistake?

Let's go swimming! In the hot time of summer, we all like most to go to swim. However, swim is not only to soak within the water to fade away the hot summer, it has more positive meaning. We pursue this meaning while we go to swim.

向日葵

只要太陽一落，黑暗一來，向日葵便垂頭閉目，不屑一顧那些齷齪事——任誰在黑暗裡活動，任誰在黑暗裡紙醉金迷，任誰在黑暗裡酒肉徵逐……。

當漫漫長夜漸次消隱，黎明漸次來臨，太陽終於以其萬丈光芒照臨大地，向日葵便抬起頭來，歡欣鼓舞了——向四面八方伸展出一瓣瓣花瓣，形成太陽的形象，以其圓形花朵，迎接太陽……。

膜拜嚮往光明，探索追求光，向日葵面向太陽英勇地挺立著，雄起起，氣昂昂……。

膜拜和嚮往是可以的，探索和追求也是必需的，只有模仿卻萬萬要不得。那是會失去自己的。創造則更必需，尤其是作家、藝術家，更需有自己在，更需要創造。試想，一個作家，一個藝術家，如果沒有自己，沒有創造，那是一則多大的笑話！

這樣說來，向日葵便是一個很有自己很有創造性的作家或藝術家了。它膜拜嚮往光明，追求光明，面向太陽英勇地挺立著，終於在大地上創造出了太陽，金黃色花瓣鑲著一枚枚真珠，閃射出萬丈光芒，成了詩人的桂冠。——而它，哦，它不也成了一名詩人？看！它創造了一枚太陽，把它當成了一頂桂冠，戴在頭上……。

詩人呀！且膜拜嚮往光明吧！且探索追求光明吧！且創造一枚太陽，如向日葵，當成一頂桂冠，戴在頭上吧！

The Sunflower

Only it's sunset, the darkness befalls, sunflower will hang its head and close its eyes, won't even spare a glance for those dirty thing-let whoever to move in the darkness, let whoever to luxury and dissipation in the darkness, let whoever to run for wine and flesh in the darkness…

When the long night fades away slowly, dawn befalls slowly, the sun eventually reflects the earth with profusion of radiance, the sunflower will lift its head, rejoice-stretches its petals forward far and near, forms the shape of sun, welcomes the sun with round flower…

Worships and longs for brilliance, searches for brilliance, sunflower brave stands erectly toward the sun, valiantly, in high spirits…

It's well for worship and long, it's need for search, but just model is intolerable absolutely. Creation is more need, especially the writer, the artist, more need has self, more need to create. Imagine, if there is no self and creation, a writer or an artist may be a joke!

So, the sunflower is a writer or an artist possesses of very creativeness. It worships and longs for brilliance, brave stands erectly toward the sun, and eventually creates a sun on the earth the golden petal inlay pearl one by one, shining with boundless radiance, and be a crown of the poet. And it, oh, isn't it to be a poet? Lo, it creates a sun, regards as a crown wears on his head…

Oh, poet, worship and long for brilliance! Search for brilliance! To create a sun, like sunflower regards as a crown, wears on your head!

荔枝

又到荔枝成熟的季節了。枝頭上的荔枝大都已成熟，顏色殷紅了。

哇！好多荔枝呀！它們纍纍垂掛著：

一顆，兩顆，十顆，百顆，千顆，萬顆……。

一串，兩串，十串，百串，千串，萬串……。

在枝頭纍纍垂掛著，那些荔枝，殷紅，碩大，圓渾，飽熟，甸實，一顆顆是真珠，一串串是珠串。哇，「紅顆真珠真可愛」！

在枝頭垂掛著，那些荔枝，彷彿是一個個少女，醉飲了梅雨和陽光調成的雞尾酒，展現出酡紅的笑臉，在枝頭迎風款款而舞。

在枝頭纍纍垂掛著，一顆顆，一串串，都沉重而欲下墜，垂彎了樹枝，越垂樹枝越彎，至將垂折。「唉，好重！」彷彿可以聽見荔枝樹這樣的嘆息。

拈取以來，剝開紅皮，把那包著的一層半透明瑪瑙膠的果子放進嘴裡，微酸甜甘的滋味便立即漫向味覺器官，以舒適美味引出所有口中的津泉。

「一騎紅塵妃子笑」，誰說「無人知是荔枝來」？必然是誰都知道的。

必然是誰都知道的，不管是垂掛在枝頭，或已摘下：

一顆，兩顆，十顆，百顆，千顆，萬顆……。

一串，兩串，十串，百串，千串，萬串……。

The Litchi

It's the season for litchi to ripe once more. The litchis on the branches are almost ripeness, red in colour.

Wow! How many litchis are there! They hang leaps of cluster after cluster:

One grain, two grains, ten grains, hundred grains, thousand grains, ten thousand grains...

One cluster, two clusters, ten clusters, hundred clusters, thousand clusters, ten thousand clusters...

Hangs leaps on the branches, those litchis, red, large, round, full, the pearl one after another, the pearl one cluster after another cluster. Wow, "How lovable the red pearl"!

Hang on, those litchis like young girl one after another, drunk cocktail into intoxicated, appears the redden smile, faces the wind to dance sincerely on the branches.

Hangs leaps on the branches, one grain after another grain, a cluster after another cluster, are heavy being to dropping down, droop bent the branch, the more droop the more the branch bent, to be break. " Alas, More heavy!" It seems the sigh of the litchi can be heard.

Pluck one, peel the red shell, put fruit included a layer of half-transparent gem into mouth, immediately the taste of little sour plus sweet roams over organ of sense of taste, leads out all of the saliva with dainty.

"A horse loads the man carry litchis made imperial concubine smile", who says "no one knows it's the litchi arrived"? Surely, it must be known by everybody.

Surely, it must be known by everybody, in spite of it hangs on the branch or is plucked:

One grain, two grains, ten grains, hundred grains, thousand grains, ten thousand grains...

One cluster, two clusters, ten clusters, hundred clusters, thousand clusters, ten thousand clusters...

稻子成熟時

　　時序進入五月，田裡處處可見，稻子成熟了。

　　時光飛逝，快如閃電，田裡的稻子彷彿才種下，竟然已出穗成熟了。稻穗一穗穗垂掛著，一穗穗長滿飽熟纍纍的穀粒，垂彎了稻株。在金陽的明照下，一顆顆飽熟的穀粒，閃出金黃的光芒，是一顆顆珠顆，把一穗穗稻穗串成一串串珠串。

　　小時候，懵懵懂懂，迷迷糊糊，大多滿腦子英雄崇拜思想，喜歡稻子高舉劍葉，直豎而立，給看成舉劍闊步意氣風發的英雄，風範絕世，不可一世，致有高傲表現。

　　「要學習稻子！稻子出穗成熟便垂下頭，是多麼謙卑自抑！人也該如此：你的年歲越大經驗越多人越成熟，便要越謙卑自抑，不可驕傲自滿，昂然不可一世！」

　　那時年紀小，不知道話中有真意，根本不理不睬；但是越長大便越覺得有道理。

　　隨著歲月的增加

　　頭便越垂越低下

　　哈，一個謙謙君子呀

　　是的，隨著歲月的增加頭便越垂越低下；因為成熟了！稻子這樣，人也是這樣！稻子在未出穗成熟前，劍葉直豎，昂然而立，不可一世；人在未長大成熟前，輕浮不穩，撫劍疾視，目中無人；必待成熟，頭垂下，便是一個謙謙君子了。

When the Rice is ripened

The month of May comes, we can view everywhere the rice is ripened.

Time passes rapidly like the lightning, the rice as if it just planted, the ear is ripened unexpectedly. The ear hangs one tassel by one tassel, a tassel and a tassel has leapt of full grains, droops bent the trunk. A grain and a grain of full ear, shinning the golden light under the illumination of the golden sun, is a grain and a grain of pearl, strings the ear into a cluster and a cluster of pearl string.

It's muddled and dazed in the childhood of everyone, whole their head almost hero cult thinking, like the rice lifts the sword-like leave, stands straightly, looks like to be the hero who holds the sword strides with high-spirited, elegance grace out of the world, unchallengeable, and appears haughty.

"Be learned the rice! The rice will hang its head when its ear is ripened, how humble and self-restrained itself! A person ought to be as thus: The more the experience and ripened the more the year, one ought to be more humble and self-restrained of himself, don't to swell with pride, in a dignified manner unchangeable!"

At the childhood, we can't understand the true meaning of the words, haven't took a look at it anymore; but feel it's more the true the older.

The head hangs lower
Follows the year is older
Ha, what a humble gentleman

Yes, the head is lower followed the year is older; for one is ripened! The rice is so, and the same the person! Before it's ripened, the rice lifts the sword-like leave, stands straightly, unchallengeable; before he is ripened, person frivolous and unsteady, holds sword and stern looks, haven't took a look at anyone; it must be waited till to be ripened and hanged his head, then a humble gentle man he is.

看蝴蝶

　　要看蝴蝶嗎？那麼，到田野去！到草原去！到森林去！到山中去！……蝴蝶總是住在那些地方。

　　蝴蝶總是住在那些地方！不為別的。他們懼怕人類的侵犯、污染，喜歡山野，喜歡大自然，喜歡清靜，喜歡自由自在……。

　　「這不是鳳蝶嗎？」

　　「不是。」

　　「不然是什麼蝶？黃蝶？帝王蝶？灰蝶？蛇目蝶？小紋青斑蝶？……」

　　「亂猜！縱使妳把所知道的蝴蝶名稱都搬出來，也不一定猜得到。這是木葉蝶。」

　　「哇！好多呀！總有幾千隻吧！」

　　「何止呢？總在萬隻以上！」

　　「牠們停在樹上，我還不知道呢。無意間搖動一下樹，牠們竟然煙塵般驚飛起來。哇！好美的蝴蝶！」

　　真的，真美！牠們翩翩飛翔舞踴著，具有各種形狀，各種顏色，各種姿態。牠們彷彿旋舞的少女，舞步輕移，舞姿舒展，被稱為大自然的舞姬，該是沒錯的。牠們輕盈不羈，逍遙自在，是文人高士所欽羨嚮往的。莊周夢為蝴蝶，豈是偶然？

　　蝴蝶是很可一看的。且到田野去！且到草原去！且到森林去！且到山中去！……牠們總是住在那些地方。

Let's go to Watch Butterfly

Do you want to watch butterfly? Then, go to the field! Go to the grassland! Go to the forest! Go to the mountain!... Butterfly always stays those places.

Butterfly always stays those places! Not for other sake. They afraid of the invasion of the human being, pollution, love mountain area, love nature, love secluded, love leisurely and carefree...

"Is this not the papilio?"

"No."

"Or is it what kind of butterfly? The eurema hecabe? The monarch butterfly? The Lycaenidae? The satyridae? The tirumala septentronis? ..."

"Wild guess! Even if you carry all the name of the butterflies you know, is also unsettled to guess it correctly. It's the Kallima inachus."

"Wow! How nice! They may some thousands in all!"

"Far more than this. May be ten thousands in all."

"They stay on the trees, I don't know originally. They scare to fly like the smoke while I shake the tree accidentally. Wow! How beautiful the butterfly!"

True! It's beautiful truly! They fly and dance elegantly, with every shade, every colour, every posture. They like the young girl dances revolve, moves their steps slightly, the dance posture spread slightly, is no wrong to be called the dancing girl of the nature. They gentle, freely, carefree and enjoying themselves, are envied and longed by scholar and noble. Is it occasion while Zhuangzi dreams of a butterfly?

Butterfly is worth watch. Let's go to the field! Let's go to the grassland! Let's go to the forest! Let's go to the mountain!... They always stay those place.

流星

　　靜夜裡，一顆流星劃過，劃過那藍藍的夜空，劃過那深深的夜空……

　　一顆流星劃過，帶著一把燦爛的亮光……。

　　一顆流星劃過，就在現在，就在眼前……。

　　一顆流星劃過，在燦爛過一段時日後，在輝煌過一段時日後……。

　　一顆流星劃過，在我心的夜空，留下一抹光燦，一抹永恆……。

　　有很多東西是短命的，譬如朝生暮死的蜉蝣，譬如入夜才開花半夜即枯萎的曇花，還有，還有……嗨，不必還有了，人生即使活上百歲，和宇宙的千秋萬世相比，有什麼資格嘲笑蜉蝣和曇花呢？難道還不只是一瞬？

　　任你飛黃騰達，聲名赫赫，得意非凡，雄姿英發，或是窮愁潦倒，隱姓埋名，僻處一隅，鬱鬱終身，一瞬就是一瞬，又能怎樣呢？

　　時間是一滴滴水滴，在永世這條長河裡流著，一瞬，一瞬，又是一瞬……。

　　但是，只要曾經燦爛地活過，只要曾經輝煌地活過，一瞬可以是萬世，一瞬可以是不朽，一瞬可以是永恆！

　　啊，一顆流星劃過……。

The Meteor

A meteor shoots in the silent night, shoots across the blue sky, shoots across the deep night sky...

A meteor shoots, carries a bunch of brilliant light...

A meteor shoots, at present, in front of the eyes...

A meteor shoots, after it has brilliant for a period of time, after it has splendid for a period of time...

A meteor shoots, in the night sky of heart, leaves a wipe of splendid, a wipe of forever...

There are many die young in the universe, for instance, the mayfly of short life, the broad-leaves epiphyllum likes the morning dew, in addition, in addition... hi, don't need to say in addition, even life has hundred years, is there any qualification for you to compare to universe for all generations to come? Surely it doesn't mean that it just a moment?

In spite of you are highly successful in your career, in great reputation, favourite unusual, heroic posture, or poor and sad and careless and sloppy, conceal the name, live in a remote corner, melancholy whole the life, a moment is a moment, how can you do about it?

Time is water drip drop by drop, flows in the forever river, a moment, a moment, and a moment again...

However, just lived brilliantly, lived splendid, may a moment is an eternity, a moment may be immortality, a moment can be forever!

Oh, a meteor shoots...

石榴

「石榴照眼紅！」

誰說不是？只要炎夏一到，石榴便禁不住炎炎炙陽熱情的招請，盡情地綻放，綻放在枝頭，綻放出它的如火熱情，炙熱逼人，回應炎炎炙陽的熱情，綻放出它的豔紅，如一盞盞紅燈在綠原上高舉、照亮，持續幾近整整一個夏季……。

它那犬齒狀的花瓣，恰似少女穿著的裙邊，曲線玲瓏，包藏多少祕密？逗人多少遐思？具有多少男人心折拜倒的魔力？再者，古時婦女喜歡採摘它，搗碎研汁，塗布做裙，穿在身上，搖曳生姿，頓增殊多少女神祕魔力，使男人為之著迷傾倒。那就更富羅曼蒂克情味，更具傳奇性，更寫意了。嗯，是的，誰都會想起這句話的：

「拜倒石榴裙下。」

待到秋日，石榴便結果了，一顆顆垂掛枝頭，仍然展現其豔紅，展現其照眼，展現其神祕與熱情，裡面子多，真是多子多孫！爆裂時，正像一個蜂巢，一盤珍肴，一盤紅蝦，任鳥雀前來啄食，引為大餐……。

凝聚，凝聚，再凝聚，儲藏，儲藏，再儲藏，醞釀，醞釀，再醞釀，準備著要去作最佳的表現……。

啊，終於綻放了，終於呀

石榴，是的，不管它是花，是葉，都豔紅，都熱情，都神祕呀迷人……。

The Pomegranate

"The pomegranate brightens the sight."

Who says it's not? Only hot summer comes, pomegranate can not bear the invitation of the enthusiasm of the hot sun, blossoms to its heart content, blossoms on the branch, blossoms into its fire like enthusiasm, hot presses everyone, responds the enthusiasm of the hot sun, blossoms its gorgeous, like a red lamp and a red lamp lifts and brightens on the green plain, successively almost whole the season...

The dog-like teeth, just as the sideline of the skirt of the young girl, in carving the fine delicate, how many secrets does it harbours? How much far thought does it attracts? How many magic to admire by the men does it possess? More over, ancient women like to pluck it, break it into pieces, smear on the cloth to be the skirt, wear on, grace posture while wavering and swaying, add many secret magic immediately to the young girl, make men be fascinated and great admire. That is more romantic interest, more legend, more after his own heart. N, yes, whoever has heard this saying:

"Be fascinated and admired under the pomegranate skirt."

When autumn is come, pomegranate bears fruit, hangs on the branch one by one, still unfolded its secret and gorgeous, unfolded brightness, unfolded its secret and enthusiasm, many seeds within, it's truly many offspring and descendants! When bursts, it just likes a honeycomb, a plate of delicacies, a plate of shrimp, for birds to peck, to be a gourmet meal...

Condense, condense again, and condense again, preserve, preserve again, and preserve again, brew, brew again, and brew again, it prepares to do the best show...

Oh, blossom eventually, eventually

Pomegranate, yes, in spite of flower or leave, all are gorgeous, all are enthusiasm, all are secret and attract great admire...

我們來跳繩

一、二、三，我們來跳繩！

「跳增彈性的力量，

跳開歡笑的花朵，

跳成我們健壯的體格。」

要看嗎？要看什麼？看誰跳得高？看誰跳的次數多？……

何止於此？不止哪！

來！肩迴旋！肘迴旋！腕迴旋！……

來！一跳一迴旋！一跳二迴旋！二跳一迴旋！……

來！半迴旋！正迴旋！反迴旋！側迴旋！水準迴旋！……

來！單人單腳！單人雙腳！雙人單腳！雙人雙腳！多人多腳！……

哇！花樣這麼多！已是琳瑯滿目，目不暇給了。

跳繩果真是很好的運動和娛樂。看！那麼輕快靈巧！那麼美妙多姿！人在繩陣裡，就像閃飛的雀鳥。

「累嗎？」

「不會。」

那麼我們就來跳吧！

「跳離無知的坎井，

跳向廣闊的世界，

跳出一個完美無缺來。」

Let's Come to Rope Skipping

One, two, three, we come to rope skipping!
Skip to add the strength of the spring,
Skip to open the flower of the laugh with joy,
Skip to the healthy of our body.

Do you want to take a look at? What do you want to take a look at? Who skips the higher? Whom do you want to know the most number he skips?...

Does far more than this? No only this!

Lo! Conveyor of shoulder! Conveyor of elbow! Conveyor of wrist!...

Lo! One skip with one conveyor! Two conveyors with one skip! Two skips with one conveyor!...

Lo! Half conveyor! Right conveyor! Anti-conveyor! Flank conveyor! Level conveyor!...

Lo! A person with one foot! A person with two feet! Both with one foot! Two persons with two feet! Majority of person with majority of feet!...

Wow! How many patterns! It's a feast for the eyes to look with fixed eyes!

The rope skipping is really a very good exercise and amusement. Lo! How light and handy and nimble! How beautiful and colourful! A person is like the flying bird while he is in the shower of the rope.

"Do you tire?"

"No."

Then, let's skip!
Skip to leave the well of ignorance,
Skip toward the wide world,
Skip into perfection and zero defection.

海邊戲水

「海邊戲水去！」

是天太熱了吧！總聽到有人這樣的邀約，也聽到有人答應：

「好呀！走吧！」

看呀！整個海邊，好多人在戲水！在水裡，有游泳的，有泡水的，有追逐的，有相互潑水的；在沙灘上，有撿貝殼的，有抓螃蟹的，有躺在遮陽傘下的；有的則一會兒沙灘一會兒水裡奔逐戲耍……。

海浪爆開成許多花朵。笑聲爆開成許多花朵。話聲爆開成許多花朵。……

「哇！好涼爽！」

是好涼爽呀，那些海水，那些笑臉，那些歡呼！

「我抓到一隻了。」

抓到一隻什麼？螃蟹？小魚？快樂？

「我學會了。」

學會什麼？游泳？潑水？抓蟹？

……

當黃昏，他們各自歸去；他們仍然戀戀不捨。畢竟他們有那麼一段快樂的時光，在海邊戲水。他們又開始憧憬著：

「下次再來！來海邊戲水！」

Free play on seaside

"Let's free play on the seaside!"

May it be too hot! We often hear thus invitation by someone as well as promise from someone:

"Well! Let's go!"

Lo, they are many people free play on the seaside! In the water, some swimming, some soak , some chase, some sprinkle water with each other; on the sandy beach, some collect shell, some catch crab, some lay down beneath the parasol; some chase and play between sandy beach and the water…

The sprays burst forth into many flowers. The sound of laugh burst forth into many flowers. The voice of stalking burst forth into many flowers…

"Wow, how cool it is!"

It's really very cool, those sea water, those smiling face, those hail!

"I catch one."

What is he catch? crab? small fish? joyful?

" I'm master."

What is he master? Swim? Water-sprinkle? Catch crab?

… ….

When dusk falls, each back home; they are reluctant still. They have a good time free play on seaside after all. They start to long for again:

"Come once more! Come to seaside to free play on the seaside!"

美好的世界

　　一早出門，見晴空萬里，陽光普照，到處一片欣欣向榮，加上和煦的春風輕輕拂面，便覺無限舒爽，欣喜非常，肯定今天必定是一個美好的日子，這個世界必定是一個美好的世界。

　　才出門沒多久，一群學生便笑盈盈地向我揮手，大喊：「老師早！」我一一向他們道好。沿路也一再和許多熟人相互打招呼問好。他們的臉上也堆滿著笑。

　　沒多久，看見一個騎單車的小孩摔了。我立刻一個箭步過去，要把他扶起，卻有一個青年已先我而到，把他扶起來了。

　　「多謝！」

　　「摔傷了沒？」

　　「沒關係！」

　　在車上，只見有老弱婦孺上車，便有年輕人讓座。

　　「請坐！」

　　「多謝！」

　　多悅耳的對話！

　　有一群學生模樣的青年，男女都有，約廿個。我和他們談了起來，問他們哪裡去。他們說，先到老人院去慰問老人，幫他們整理房間，然後到育幼院，和院童同樂。哇，多有意義的活動！

　　在回家的路上，看見有一個青年扶著一個老人過街道。在夕陽餘暉的映照下，那個青年很有耐心地和老人，一步一步慢慢走過街道。他們的四周似乎特別亮。所有車輛到那裡，都停下來讓路。……

　　我相信，還有更多這樣美好的事，在各地進行，也不只今天，天天都有。我更相信，這是一個美好的世界。

It must be a fine world

As soon as I go out from my home, I see there is a clear and boundless sky, the sunlight shines on the whole world, flourishing everywhere, in addition to the warm breeze blows slightly, let me feel at ease limitless, very happy, affirm that it must be a fine day today, it must be a fine world.

No soon as I go out, a group of students wave their hands toward me, shout loudly: "Good morning, teacher!" I say good morning respond to everyone. And, along the road, I also call and greet each other with familiar friend time and again. Their face all full with smile.

No sooner, I find a child fell from the bicycle he rode. I go on in a shot step immediately wish to help him, but a youth has help him up.

"Thanks."

"Is there any hurt?"

"Nothing matter!"

On the bus, the youths offer their seats for the priority.

"Take a seat, please!"

"Thank you."

How pleasant to the ear the dialogue!

There is a group of youths of student-like, both male and female, about 20 on age. I talk with them, where are they going. They say they want to express sympathy and solicitude for the ages in the aged care nursing home at first, help them to sort out their house, and then go to nursery home joy together with the children. Wow, what a meaningful thing they do!

On the road back home, I view a youth help an age cross the road. I see the youth patiently and the age, step by step under the afterglow, walk across the road. It seems bright special around them. All vehicles stop there for them to go through…

I believe, there are more fine things as thus still happen everywhere, and it's not just today, it's happened every day. I believe more, this is a fine world.

微風裡

　　微風輕輕吹過，帶來一片美好。但願微風常常吹來！在微風裡真好！

　　這是一條細細的水流，緩緩地流過田野，滋潤著土地，給所有生命以愛的營養，促其順利成長，愉快生活，悠然自得。

　　這是一些輕輕的微語，出自甜蜜的嘴唇，灌溉乾枯無生意的心田，復活一片寂寂的心意之禾苗，使之充滿盎然生意。

　　這是一個可人的微笑，來自一個姣好的臉龐，配上一雙脈脈的眼睛，激起心湖中圈圈愛的漣漪，一圈接著一圈，久久不停。

　　這是一種適意的蜜糖，來自甘蔗，來自蜜蜂，解除乾渴的心靈，除去苦澀，驅走羸弱，培養平和，帶來強健和舒爽。

　　這是一片冬天的太陽，在凜冽的寒冬裡，帶來一團溫暖，驅去所有寒冷、陰霾、濃霧，闢出一個光亮、溫熱的世界。

　　這是一個美好的春天。寒冷的冬天已過，春陽正來到人間，冬眠的動物已醒轉，植物已萌芽。好個溫暖、生氣蓬勃的日子！

　　微風輕輕吹過，帶來一片美好。但願微風常常吹來！在微風裡真好！

In the Breeze

The breeze blows gently, brings a scene of fine feeling. Wishing the breeze often blows! It's really good in the breeze!

It's a fine stream, flows slowly into the field, moist the soil, sends to all the life with nutrition of love, promotes them to grow up, lives happily, in an easy manner and self-satisfied.

It's a thin voice, offers from the sweet lips, waters the mind field of dry up out of vigour and vitality, revives the young paddy of empty mind, let it be full of abundant vigour and vitality.

It's a happy smile, comes from a pretty face, companies with a pair of affectionate eyes, arouse the ripples of love, a ring after a ring, long ceaselessly.

It's an agreeable honey, comes from sugarcane, comes from honeybee, removes thirsty of the mind, drives away bitter and harsh to the taste, drives away the weak, trains the peace, brings the healthy and comfortable.

It's a piece of sunshine in winter, brings a group of warmth in the chilly winter, drives all the cold, gloomy, dense fog, builds a bright and warm world.

It's a fine spring. The cold winter is over, the spring sun is coming, the hibernated animal is awoken, the plants are sprouted. What a warm and flourishing day!

The breeze blows gently, brings a scene of fine feeling. Wishing the breeze often blows! It's really good in the breeze!

星星

　　星星，閃爍著，這裡一顆，那裡也一顆，在天際，在深邃的天際……

　　星星，一顆顆，是一朵朵花，盛放的，舒展的，花枝高高攀舉而起。一瓣瓣花瓣是一個個生命，叢集一起，組成一朵朵美，予平淡添上生動，把大地這張畫紙點畫上多彩多姿……。

　　星星，一顆顆，是一口口井，滿儲著泉水，隨意汲取，以飲，則涓涓滴滴，涼爽甘美，極為可口，可以解除焦渴，以洗，則潔淨無垢，可以滌除汙穢，帶來清新，帶來涼爽……。

　　星星，一顆顆，是一朵朵微笑，綻放在孩童的臉上，綻放在有情人的臉上，是那麼天真無邪，是那麼無拘無束，是那麼甜美迷人，是那麼引人入勝，在枯燥的生活之汪汪大海中，吹起漣漪，掀起小小浪花，帶來甜蜜、快樂和美滿……。

　　星星，一顆顆，是一隻隻美人的明眸，盈盈溢溢，充滿了深情的，充滿了透視的力量的，只要美目輕輕一盼，便足以懾人心魂，便足以直接透入人的心靈深處，照拂所有各個角落，讓心靈深處大放光明，任何一絲陰暗或陰翳一掃而光……。

　　星星，閃爍著，這裡一顆，那裡也一顆，在天際，在深邃的天際……。

Stars

Stars, one is here, one is there, twinkling in the sky, in the deep sky...

Stars, one by one, are a flower and a flower, full open, unfold, the twig high climb. A petal and a petal is one life and one life, be overgrows into one beauty and one beauty, adds flat into vivid, paints the paper of the earth into colourful...

Stars, one by one, are a well and a well, full stores the spring, derives at will, for drink, the tiny drop may cool and sweet, great in tasty, can drive thirsty, for wash, may clean and tidy without stain, can wash away dirty, bring fresh, bring the cool...

Stars, one by one, are a smile and a smile, full open on child's face, full open on lovers' face, is so innocent without evil, so unrestrained, so sweet and bewitch, so fascinating, on large ocean of the dull and dry life, stirs some ripples, arouses small sprays, send sweet, happy and very satisfactory...

Stars, one and one, are the eyes of the beauty, full and overflow, holds deep passionate, holds power to penetration, only take a sight by her bright eyes, will frighten the heart of others, will penetrate through into the deep heart, brighten all corners make the deep heart full of light, any gloomy or haze will all sweep out...

Stars, one is here, one is there, in the sky, in the deep sky...

走進山裡

山時時在召喚我。

我走進山裡。

山裡有高崖，有谿谷，有澗泉，有瀑布，有森林⋯⋯。

山崖有時是高聳而陡峭的，彷彿造物以神劍劈削出來的，是那麼陡，那麼直，那麼巧奪天工；與深深谿谷相比，每有天淵之別。

走啊走，可能就碰到澗泉了。澗泉，流遍整座山，時緩時急，時大時小，不停地流著，潺潺琮琮地唱著，讓歌聲傳遍山林⋯⋯。

沿澗泉而上，欲「行到水窮處」，總有碰到瀑布的機會。瀑布啊，在那裡曝曬她的金銀珠寶呀！除閃發金光銀光而外，還碰出嘩啦啦叮叮噹噹的聲音呢！

或高或矮，或大或小，山裡有樹，成群，成片，成林，為山製造著青翠、涼蔭和新鮮空氣，召來禽鳥飛鳴棲息其間，獸類蹦躍、寢食、活動其間⋯⋯。

在山裡，隨時隨地有美麗的風景好觀賞，有新鮮的空氣好呼吸，有怡人的清靜好享受，有大自然的奧祕好探究⋯⋯。

走進山裡，走進一重山又一重山，去享受山的盛宴，去探訪大自然的奧祕⋯⋯。

走進山裡，我走進山裡。

Enter the mountain

The mountain summons me very often.

And I enter the mountain.

There is cliff, valley, brook, falls and forest in the mountain…

Sometimes the cliff is cliffy, as if it's the Creator split it with god sword, is so sharp, so straight, so fine workmanship; often it is as far apart as heaven from earth while compares with the deep valley.

Go as we please, we may meet the brook. The brook, flows all over the mountain, sometimes flows slowly, sometimes hurriedly, ceaselessly, sings murmuring and gurgling, spreads its song all over the mountain and forest…

Go along the brook, if wish to go to "the beginning of the water", you always have the opportunity to meet the falls. The falls, expose to the sun its treasures just as gold, silver, pearl etc.! Except to shine the light of gold and silver, besides to bump the sound of walla-walla and ding-dong!

Either high or low, either big or small, in the mountain, there are trees, may in group, in piece, in forest, make green, cool shade and fresh air for the mountain, summon the birds to sing and perch among them, beasts to leap, feed and sleep and operate among them…

In the mountain, there is beautiful scenery at any time and everywhere for you to view, fresh air for you to breathe, cheerful quiet for you to enjoy, secret of nature for you to make a through inquiry…

Enter the mountain, enter a pile and a pile of mountain, to enjoy the grand banquet of the mountain, to make a through inquiry…

Enter the mountain, I enter the mountain.

浪花

　　到海邊，總會看到海水激起許多或大或小的白色浪花。是由海水激盪而成的，有時候海水激盪得厲害，竟至波濤洶湧，白浪滔天，有如千堆雪，非常壯觀，引人不少遐思，給人不少啟示。

　　人間浮世，不就是一片汪洋大海？既是汪洋大海，何得而不有浪花？是的，有，不但有，而且相當大，每每還洶湧澎湃，非常壯觀呢！

　　以我國來說，自盤古開天闢地起，歷經多少變化而秦、漢、唐、宋、元、明、清，以至而今，其間有多少美麗的浪花激濺而起？那些浪花一定包括了漢、滿、蒙、回、藏、苗、徭等等民族的血汗！較特出的怕是春秋、戰國時代、五胡亂華、魏晉南北朝、三國時代、佛教的傳入、明清的東西交通吧！而最多最強最大最烈的便是現代人，總是相激相盪，怒潮澎湃，白浪滔天，有如千堆雪。

　　原來人間浮世，人心之不同各如其面，各人站在各自的立場和角度，所見不同，自有紛爭。紛爭並不可怕，如果能從紛爭中相互激盪、溝通、融合，得出新的結果，可能更好。它會是一股更大的力量，足以衝破重重艱難，創造新的史頁。要做到這境地，必需有開放的環境，各人也要有開放的胸襟，時常想到別人的立場，心平氣和相待。

　　那麼，就開放出環境，開放出胸襟吧！時常想到別人的立場，化紛爭為力量吧！這樣，紛爭的浪花必會壯觀！

The Spray

We always can see many white sprays big or small aroused by the sea water in the seaside. They are stirred by the seawater, sometimes the seawater stirred severely, even surge into great wave, white breakers leaping up to the sky, as thousand piles of snow, grand and impressive in sight, leads us to be lost in reverie, leads us many inspiration.

Isn't it the mortal world a vast boundless ocean? As it's a vast boundless ocean, why is it not the spray? Yes, it is. Not only it is, it's also somewhat large, it often surging still, and very grand and impressive sight.

As to our country, since the dawn of history from Pan Gu, experienced how many changes to Chin, Han, Tang, Song, Yuan, Ming, Qing, till now, are they stirred how many sprays among them? Those sprays must be included the blood and sweat of Han, Manchu, Mongols, Hui people, Tibetan people, Miao people, Yao people etc.! The more outstanding things are the time of The Eastern Zhou period, The Uprising of the Five Barbarians, The Northern and Southern dynasties, the Three Kingdoms, the circulation of Buddhism, the communication of western and eastern cultures in time of Ming and Qing! And the most strong and violent is the modern who often surging each other, angry waves surge high, white-crested waves surging and swelling sky-high as thousand piles of snow.

Originally, on the mortal world, the diffident mind of person just as their appearances, everyone stands on his viewpoint and position, different as they view, of course there may bring dissention. It doesn't to be fearful, it may better after the new result is come from the surging, communication and melt from the dissention. It will be a larger power, enough to break through problems layer after layer, create new page of history. Want to arrive this boundary, we must hold the opening circumstance, each one also has the open mind, often thinks of other's position, treats to another with peaceful.

Then, open the circumstance, open the mind! Often think of other's position, turn dissention into power! Thus, the spray of the dissention must be grand and impressive in sight!

快樂早晨

　　昨夜一覺到天亮，睡好睏足，疲勞盡褪；今晨早起，但覺一身清爽，體力充沛，精神飽滿，欣喜非常。

　　探首窗外，穹蒼萬里無雲，無盡碧藍，弓向高遠。一片青翠在微曛中鋪展而出，是一塊無限大的綠色絨毯，迎接清晨的喜悅。

　　我遂走向屋外……。

　　假日，不必趕上班，可以不受時間拘束，要舉步向哪裡便舉步向哪裡，要神遊多久就神遊多久。

　　清風徐來，圍繞著我直轉，時而在前，時而在後，時而在左右，送來輕輕撫觸，送來無限清爽，送來鄉土的芬芳……。

　　或遠或近，或大或小，或高或低，鳥鳴蟲唱陣陣傳來，清脆的，輕盈的，巧囀的。是獨唱？是合唱？是齊唱？是輪唱？……想是歌頌這個快樂早晨吧！

　　晶瑩的露珠在草木的葉尖閃著亮光。好不忍地踩上去，一陣陣清涼從赤裸的腳底直傳內心深處。哇！好清涼呀！夏日的燠熱不再。真的是個快樂早晨！

　　旭日東升，灑下萬丈光芒，象徵年輕蓬勃朝氣，象徵前程一片光明，無限希望……。

　　當我回來，我帶回了徐徐清風、鳥鳴、蟲唱、露珠、清爽、光明、希望……。

　　啊，一個快樂早晨！

The merry morning

I slept well last night, had a sweet and sound sleep, all tiresomeness is slipped out; got up this morning, I feel just fresh, full of physical strength, as well as the spirit, very joyful.

Look out of the window, there aren't any cloud in the wide azure, blue limitless, bows toward high and far. A piece of green spreads on the dim light of the dawn, is a piece carpet of boundless, welcome the joy of the cool dawn.

I then go toward the outdoors…

It's a holiday, I needn't hurry to go to work, can't restrain by time, may go wherever I want, can wander how long what I want…

Cool breeze blows slightly, makes turn around me ceaselessly, sometimes before me, sometimes behind me, sometimes on my sides, sends me the gentle touch, sends me the cool limitless, sends the sweet-smelling of the native land…

Either far or near, either big or small, either high or low, the song of bird and insect spreads spell by spell, light and handy, gentle, tangling. Is it the solo? Choir? Concerted singing? Or a round?… Most probably it's eulogized of the merry morning!

The crystal dew shines the light on the blade of the grass and tree. I can't bear to tread on them, a spell and a spell of coolness transmit into my deep heart from my bare feet. Wow, how cool it is! The scorched hot of summer is no more. It's really a merry morning!

The rising sun sprinkles radiance with boundless indignation, symbolizes young and vitality and flourishing, symbolizes there is a piece of light in the future, hope limitless…

When I back home, I bring with the cool breeze, the song of bird and insect, dew, coolness, light, hope…

Oh, what a merry morning!

迎向藍天

迎向藍天，迎向雲間，迎向曠野，我們冉冉飛起，冉冉飛起……。

冉冉飛起，冉冉飛起……漸漸高起了，漸漸遠離地面了……。

地面上的人物漸漸變小了，漸漸模糊了。人成了螞蟻。車輛成了火柴盒。樓房成了疊著的積木。道路是腰帶。河流是衣服的花邊。……

我們向前飛行著，依循一定的軌道。

窗外是一片藍天，一片藍天又一片藍天，向四面八方擴展而去，向四面八方又向四面八方擴展而去，是那麼蔚藍亮麗，那麼蔚藍亮麗又那麼蔚藍亮麗，一片空曠渺遠，空曠渺遠又空曠渺遠，無有盡處……。

藍天裡，或遠或近，這裡那裡，有著雲。雲，有些是濃厚的，有些是稀薄的，有些是孤單獨存的，有些是連綿成群的，有些是這個形狀，有些是那個形狀，都因水氣、溫度和風的不同變化而定。至於雲的顏色，則大都是黑白的，偶爾也有彩色的。

我們向前飛行著，向前飛行，又向前飛行……。

好平穩！好舒適！比在地面上坐車還平穩舒適！

穿進雲裡，窗外便是一片模糊，一片棉花糖……。

穿出雲外，窗外便是一片蔚藍，一片亮麗……。

向前飛行，又向前飛行，我們向前飛行……。

In Face of Azure

In face of azure, in face of cloud, in face of open field, we hover slowly, hover slowly...

Hover slowly, hover slowly... higher gradually, far from the land surface gradually...

Becomes small one after another the persons and things on the land surface, and dim one after another. Person becomes the ant. Vehicle becomes the match box. Manson becomes toy bricks overlapping. Road is the waist-belt. River is the lace of the garment...

We hover forward, according to a fixed track.

It's the azure outside the window, a piece of azure and a piece of azure, spread toward all directions, spread toward all direction and all directions, is thus blue and bright, thus blue and bright and thus blue and bright, a stretch spacious and distant remove, a stretch of spacious and distant remove and a stretch of spacious and distant remove, boundless...

In the azure, there are clouds hither and thither, either far or near. The clouds, some are thick, some are thin, some are standing alone, some are in group successively, some are in that shape, some are in this shape, are decided by the changes of the steam, temperature and wind. As to the colour of the cloud, often are black and white, some are colourful occasionally.

We hover forward, hover forward, and hover forward once again...

How steady it is! How cozy it is! It's more steady and cozy than on the vehicle on the road!

Pierce into the cloud, outside the window is a piece of dim, a piece of cotton candy...

Hover outside the cloud, out of the window is a piece of blue, a piece of bright...

Hover forward, also hover forward, we hover forward...

森林的早晨

晨曦從東方漸次移來，帶來光明。

森林裡，野獸、昆蟲、禽鳥和草木漸次甦醒過來了，帶來了熱鬧。

「喂！起床了！」那是白兔媽媽喊的，要把小白兔寶寶喊醒。

「早安！」此起彼落，到處有這聲音響起。是森林裡的野獸、昆蟲、禽鳥和草木醒來了，第一次見面，便相互這麼招呼著。好親切！

漸漸地，有歌聲響起了。演唱的曲子是「森林的早晨」。最先是白頭翁起的音，漸次加入了烏鶖、斑鳩、青苔鳥、白翎鷥、黃鶯等禽鳥的，也漸次加入了螻蛄、紡織娘、蟋蟀等昆蟲的，還有松鼠、山鹿、白兔、羚羊等野獸的。這是一支交響曲，由天籟組成，此呼彼應，或高或低，或強或弱，節拍明快，曲調輕靈，悅耳動聽。

不管是野獸，是昆蟲，是禽鳥，是草木，都精神飽滿，表情愉快，滿臉笑容，眼睛閃著明亮的光芒，行動敏捷，看起來全身是勁。

全身是勁才好呀！這樣才顯得活潑、強壯，前途無量，光明在望。

是的，光明在望！太陽漸漸昇高起來了。它把光芒撒遍了整個森林。到處都顯得光明燦亮。

野獸、昆蟲、禽鳥和草木，各自開始了自己的工作。

The Morning of the Forest

The first flush of dawn moves slowly from east, brings the light.

In the forest, the animals, insects, birds and grasses and trees are awaking one after another, brings slowly the light.

"Hello, Get up please!" Calling the mother of white hare, wishes to call awaken her babies.

"Good morning!" Rise here and subside there, this sound resounds everywhere. Thus call each other the first meeting while the beasts, insects, birds and grasses and trees awakened. How cordial the talk!

Slowly, the songs rise. What they play is "Morning of the Forest". The first attack is the light-vented bulbul, then in turn to the birds as black drongo, turtle-dove, Japanese white-eye, egret, oriole etc., and also in turn to the insects as mole cricket, katydid, cricket etc., in addiction to the beasts as squirrel, deer, hare, antelope etc.. This is a symphony, composed by sounds of nature, chime in with each other, either high or low, either strong or weak, clear and lively in metre, slim and graceful in tune, melodious is pleasant to the ear.

Whether the beasts, insects, birds or grasses and trees, they all full of beans, cheerful countenance, full smile on face, shine the bright radiance in their eyes, agile in action, look like vividly whole the body.

It's good vividly whole the body. It appears lively, strong, future is limitless, bright future is catch sight of.

Yes, bright future is catch sight of. The sun high rises slowly. It spreads the radiance whole the forest. There appears brilliance everywhere.

The beast, insect, bird and grass and tree start their work each other.

走進山林

走進山林裡，在那個天清氣朗的日子。

只為了要走進山林裡，便走進山林裡。

走進山林裡，有許多愉悅在心頭。

古人造字，多有意思！樹，一棵是木，兩棵成林，三棵以上便成森。山裡多樹，一棵棵聚集成叢，綿延成片，統合為森林，渲染出綠，遮覆成蔭，綠遍群山，蔭覆群山；偶爾有陽光從枝葉間被篩下，是碎珠濺玉！

走進山林裡，被染得滿身是綠。

走進山林裡，被灑得滿身是蔭。

有鳥雀鳴唱飛翔其間。有走獸奔跑追逐其間。有清風吹拂蹦語其間。……

「聽，多悅耳的鳥鳴！」

「多輕巧的鳥兒呀！」

「鳥兒自由地飛翔，多悠遊自在！」

「好可愛的小鹿！」

「清風徐來，好涼爽！」

……

長長地吸口氣，用力地吐出。哇，好舒暢！如果能常在山林裡多好！可是不行的。即使依依不捨，依依不捨又能如何？還是要離開的。

就這樣，離開了山林。

離開了山林。心中還戀著山林。

Enter Mountain Forest

Enter mountain forest on the reddish black fine day.

Just for want to enter mountain forest, I enter mountain forest.

There are a large amount of joys in my mind while enter mountain forest. How meaningful the ancients created the characters. Tree, one is a wood, two becomes to tree, above three becomes to forest. There are many trees in the mountain, one and one get together into tussock, extends into piece, and to be called forest by joint, enormously exaggerates into green, covers into shade, green all over group of the mountain, shade covers group of the mountain; occasionally there are the sunshine sieve down from the branches and leaves, it's the flying pearls and splashing jade!

Enter mountain forest, full of my body is dyed into green.

Enter mountain forest, my body is splashed into damp and cool!

There are birds singing and flying among them. There are beasts running and chasing among them. There are cool breeze blowing and murmuring among them…

"Lo, how sweet-sounding the bird's vocalization!"

"How light and handy the birds!"

"How leisure fly freely of the birds!"

"How lovely the fawn!"

"The cool breeze blows gently, how cool it is!"

… …

Inhale in long, and breathe out with exhaustion. Wow, how relaxed! How fine if I can long stay in mountain forest! But it's impossible. I must leave still, even I'm reluctant to part from, what can I do about reluctant to part from?

Thus, I leave mountain forest. Though I leave mountain forest, I miss mountain forest still.

走向大自然

　　讓我們走向大自然！

　　走向大自然，哇，多麼美好！

　　大自然裡有許多美景，許多音樂，許多寶藏，許多奧祕，許多求之不盡的知識……。

　　造物是一名最精良的畫家，在大自然裡畫著，一筆一畫，一勾一勒，彩畫得均勻、和諧、多彩，成為其大無比的畫幅，是大地畫、大壁畫和天際畫的大綜合。

　　造物是一名最有才華的音樂家，能作曲，能演奏，也能歌唱，為大自然作曲、演奏、歌唱。那是一支大自然交響曲，天籟，銜接永恆，隨時間以俱存。

　　造物是一名搜羅最廣最精的收藏家，以其銳利的眼光，為大自然搜尋、鑑別各種真珠、寶玉、鑽石、古玩等等寶物，予以妥善收藏。

　　造物是一名最睿智的聖哲，把宇宙間的各種奧祕、神奇、萬有的根源和至理名言，予以窮理貫通，成為哲理，隱藏於大自然各處。

　　造物是一名最偉大的作家，充滿愛心，以其詩筆，為大自然寫下綺麗的文字，美的詩章，字字珠璣，句句雋永，篇篇可誦。

　　走向大自然，哇，多麼美好！

　　走向大自然，去欣賞美景，聆聽音樂，玩味寶藏，沉思哲理，享受文學……。

Going to the Nature

Let's go to the nature!

Go to the nature, wow, how fine it is!

In the nature, there are many scenery, several music, many treasures, many secrets, several knowledge we can't strive for…

Creator is a superior painter, painting in the nature, a pen and a draw, an outline and a cynosure, painting into even, harmonious, colourful, to be a painting the biggest of the world, is the great sum up of the paint of the earth, grant wall paint and sky paint.

Creator is a musician of the best man of unusual talent, can write music, can play, as well as sing, write music, play and sing for nature. It's a symphony of great nature, sounds of nature, links to the eternal, coexists with time.

Creator is a collector who collected at the most, collected and distinguished the treasures as pearl, jade, diamond, curio etc. with his keen eye, and well stored them.

Creator is an intelligent saint, takes hold of the secret, magical, source of the universe and axiom, to end the philosophic theory thoroughly, to be philosophic theory, hide in everywhere of the nature.

Creator is a great writer, full of compassion, writes down the elegant words into beautiful poems with his poetry pen, each word a gem, each sentence meaningful, each piece can be recited.

Go to the nature, wow, how fine it is!

Let's go to the nature, to appreciate the beautiful scenery, to listen the music, to appreciate the treasure, to ponder the philosophy, to enjoy the literary…

桂花

「啊，好香呀！」

「這是桂花呀！」

這是誰的驚讚？可能是你的，可能是他的，也可能是我的，在秋天。

在秋天，桂花總給人們帶來許多芳香，許多舒適，許多驚喜和讚美。

是的，桂花總是在秋天開放的。

當眾多花草樹木枯萎凋零，卻只有桂花開放，而且其香無匹，多麼令人驚奇！

一朵朵小花，一粒粒米粒般大小，竟會有那麼大的力量，散放出芳香，而且其香無匹，多麼令人驚奇！

莫非所有養分都集中到這裡來了。莫非所有精力都儲放到這裡來了。

它是經過多少辛苦，多少磨練，凝聚多少內力，才造成如此美好的芳香的？

別以為嬌小，力量便不大。精練、凝聚才是重要的。只要能精練、凝聚，其力量是不可小覷的。

「啊，好香呀！」

「桂花真香呀！」

精練吧！凝聚吧！精練、凝聚的工夫是多麼重要呀！精練、凝聚所得的便都是天地之間的精華。

The Sweet Olive

"Wow, how sweet it is!"

"It's the sweet olive!"

Is it whose praise? May it's yours, it's his, and it's mine, in autumn.

Yes. The sweet olive always opens in autumn.

When all flower, grass and tree wither and is bared, only the sweet olive opens, its fragrance is unmatched, how wonderful it is!

One pretty flower after one pretty flower, like little rice, has thus a great power, sprays the sweet, and its fragrance is unmatched, how wonderful it is!

Could it be that the nutrition are collected together there. Could it be that the power is stored there.

How much toilsome, how much temper has it experienced, and how much inner power coagulation has it, made this fine fragrance as such?

Don't presume that it's pretty, the power may little. Refine, coagulation is the most important thing. Just refine, coagulation, the power can't ignore.

"Wow, how sweet it is!"

"It's the sweet olive!"

To refine! To coagulation! The work of refine and coagulation is very importance! The gain of refine and coagulation is the essence between heaven and earth.

曙光已現

　　曙光終於從東方而來，展現其美姿，千萬道光芒齊放，照遍大地，帶來無限光明。顯然，夜已經逸去，白天已經降臨。

　　哇！一個紅冬冬的嬰兒終於出生了。他是經過母親十月懷胎孕育而成的。他以一聲聲輕脆的嬰啼，叩敲萬物的心扉，為大地激發新生力量，將在眾目矚視下，不停漸次成長。

　　哇！一個淪落的人終於迷途知返，浪子回頭了。他曾經走在茫茫天涯路上，徬徨，失意，不知所止，甚至和不三不四的人鬼混，為非作歹，終於犯罪，一旦翻然悔悟，迷途知返，浪子回頭，將重新做人，重獲新生。

　　哇！他終於成功了。為了完成那件事，他曾經絞盡腦汁，全心投入，流血流汗；但是經過多少打擊，遭遇多少挫折、困頓，他仍堅定意志，不為所屈，愈挫愈奮，終於有了成功的這一天。

　　哇，他終於病癒出院了。那一場大病，折磨得他好苦。但是，他信心十足，憑著醫師的藥物和他堅定的信心，可以治好他的病，使他很快便復原。現在，他病癒出院，將踏上新的路。

　　曙光終於從東方而來，展現其美姿，千萬道光芒齊放，照遍大地，帶來無限光明。顯然，夜已經逸去，白天已經降臨。我有無限欣喜。

Dawn is Appeared

Eventually, dawn comes from east, unfolds his beautiful posture, shines his radiance interrelated innumerable ways, illuminates earth, brings the bright limitless. Obviously, the night is lost, and the day is befallen.

Wow, an all red baby is born eventually. He is formed by pregnant ten months within his mother's belly. He knocks the heart of everything in the world with one and one of light baby cry, stirs new power of the earth, will be growing gradually ceaseless under the eyes watching.

Wow, realized his errors and mended his ways at last, the prodigal has returned. He once wandered at a loss on the remotest corner of the earth, hesitated about which way to go, is frustrated, knowing no abode, even led an aimless existence with indecent person, did evils, committed crimes finally, as soon as he saw the errors of his ways and repented, realized his errors and mended his ways, the prodigal has returned, he will renew behave himself, and will newborn.

Wow, he is success. In order to finish that thing, he thought over and over, put in with all his heart, shed blood and sweat; experienced how many strikes, met with how many frustration and in straitened circumstances, he still firmed his determination, don't to be subjected, the more brave the more frustration, eventually there comes a day of success.

Wow, he recovers from sickness. It was a heavy sickness. It was a serious sickness, was afflicted him into great torment. However, he full of out-and-out confidence, relies on the medicine of the doctor and his firm confidence, healed his sickness, let him recover quickly. Now, his sickness is healed and left the hospital, will step on a new road.

Eventually, dawn comes from east, unfolds his beautiful posture, shines his radiance interrelated innumerable ways, illuminates earth, brings the bright limitless. Obviously, the night is lost, and the day is befallen. I'm great pleasure limitless.

雞冠花

雞冠花，盛開得鮮紅豔麗，燦爛非常，花團錦簇，多像一朵朵大公雞頂上的肉冠！

不知道雞冠花是大公雞幻化的？抑大公雞是雞冠花幻化的？

彷彿，那是大公雞在咯咯而叫，在籬畔，在溪邊，在樹下，在園裡……。

彷彿，那是大公雞在喔喔而啼，在將黎明時，在風雨如晦之中……。

彷彿，那是大公雞披著滿身多彩的羽毛，高高翹起尾羽和翅羽……。

彷彿，那是大公雞在逡巡，在奔逐，在挺立，雄赳赳，氣昂昂……。

彷彿，那是大公雞頂上的肉冠，繫縛著英武、亢奮、勇毅和歡愉……。

彷彿，那是詩人頭上戴著朱紅桂冠，搖頭擺腦地朗聲吟誦他的詩……。

雞冠花，盛開得鮮紅豔麗，花團錦簇，多像一朵朵大公雞頂上的肉冠！

不知道雞冠花是大公雞幻化的？抑大公雞是雞冠花幻化的？

The Cockscomb

The cockscomb, blossoms into bright red and splendid, very brilliant, gorgeous spectacle, how like is it a flower and a flower of the comb on the top of the big cock!

I don't know is it the cockscomb changes from the big cock? Or is it the big cock changes from the cockscomb?

As if, it's the big cock squeaking, at the boundary of the fence, by the stream side, under the tree, in the garden…

As if, it's the big cock crows, in the dawn, in wind and rain darken the sky…

As if, it's the cock drapes over its whole body with colourfull plumes, raises its tail feature and wing feature…

As if, it's the cock patrolling, running quickly, erecting, valiantly, high moral…

As if, it's the comb on the top of the big cock, ties with martial, stimulated, courage and cheerful…

As if, it's the poet wears the vermillion red laurel, recites his poem wags his head smugly…

The cockscomb, blossoms into bright red and splendid, very brilliant, gorgeous spectacle, how like is it a flower and a flower of the comb on the top of the big cock!

I don't know is it the cockscomb changes from the big cock? Or is it the big cock changes from the cockscomb?

蟬

蟬，盡情地鳴唱著，在枝葉間。

成長是一件不容易的事，要正常地成長，要長得壯碩、健康，更不容易。不是嗎？蟬是最好的例子。牠深藏土裡，過著暗無天日的生活，一日，一月，一年……甚至十七年。

隱忍，隱忍，再隱忍；

摸索，摸索，再摸索；

修煉，修煉，再修煉；

一旦成長，牠便爬上枝葉間，大聲地鳴唱。

蟬這種小昆蟲，雖然只餐風飲露，不食人間煙火，鳴唱起來卻是頂嚴肅認真的。牠總是在枝葉間，盡其所能地鳴唱，用盡全心力地鳴唱，至死不渝。

是的，至死不渝，即使生命不長，只要嚴肅認真地鳴唱，盡其所能地鳴唱，用盡全心力地鳴唱，至死不渝，便無可遺憾了。

對整個宇宙生命來說，個人的生命只是其一瞬，也是渺小得微不足道的。在這短短的一瞬間，如何獻出自己，拿出力量為社會國家做些有益的事，為宇內增添一些光熱，是很需要的。力量也許微薄，但總比沒有好。

而且，要像蟬，不計生命的長短，用盡全心力，努力工作，不停地工作，至死不渝。

是的，至死不渝！

The Cicada

The cicada, sings to its heart's content, among the branch.

Grow up isn't an easy thing, more isn't easy to grow up in normal, to grow up strong and healthy. Isn't it? The cicada is the best sample. He hides deeply in the soil, spends his days dark as hell, a day, a month, a year..., even seventeen years.

Forbear, forbear, forbear again

Grope, grope, grope again

Temper, temper temper again

As soon as it grows up, it will climb on to the branch, sings loudly.

The cicada such a tiny insect, although only endures the hardships of traveling, lives in vain as immortal, it will very severely and seriously in singing. It always on the branch, sings as its best, sings to make all-out effort, not stop till death.

Yes, not stop till death, even its life is no long, just severely and seriously in singing, sings as its best, sings to make all-out effort, not stop till death, it's not regret.

As to life of whole universe, the life of individual only in the twinkling of an eye, is also insignificant. At this short moment, how to devote yourself, to do some benefit thing to society and country with your force, add to the universe some light and warmth, is very necessary. May be the force is little, but is better than there is no.

And, must like the cicada, not haggle long or short of the life, to make all-out effort, works hard, works ceaselessly, not stop till death.

Yes, not stop till death!

訪遊去

　　訪遊去！到名勝古蹟訪遊去！

　　訪遊去！整天整年躲在室內，是會悶壞了的，需要去鬆散鬆散一下自己。

　　訪遊去！書上的知識無法滿足人的心靈需要。到名勝古蹟訪遊，可以擴大知識的領域，以實際行動獲得第一手資料。

　　訪遊去！文化是人類生活經驗的總和，是自古至今綿延不斷，點點滴滴匯聚而成的。它是個縱剖面。其詳細的橫切面則存在古蹟裡。訪遊古蹟，可以沉浸深入古時當代的橫切面，去觀賞當時的風俗習慣，撿拾當時的遺跡，點數先人的腳印，得到許多先人的智慧結晶，獲知先人奮鬥的艱辛，心生感激，思所以承先啟後。

　　訪遊去！大自然是一本讀之不盡、訪之有餘的大書，由造物的妙筆寫成的，比任何一本用文字寫成的書都博大精深；名勝則為其抽樣。不管是名山，是大川，不論是山水，是花草樹木，都有造物的妙諦在，潛藏的智慧在。去訪遊，去細讀，可以得到大自然的妙趣，滿足心靈對知識的渴念，平撫心中的皺紋，掃除心中的陰霾。

　　訪遊去！到名勝古蹟訪遊去！

　　訪遊去！尤其是春天到了，天氣溫暖，和風送爽，風光明媚，百花盛開，鳥語花香，正是最好的訪遊時候。去吧！訪遊去！

Let's go to visit

Let's go to visit! Let's go to visit scenic spot and historic spot!

Let's go to visit! Hide in home all day long whole year long will be in the sulks, to relax yourself is necessary.

Let's go to visit! The knowledge on book can't satisfy mind's need of a person. To go to visit scenic spot and historic spot can enlarge the field of knowledge, obtain first means with real action.

Let's go to visit! Culture is the sum of human's life experience, extends ceaselessly from ancient to now, collected by drop and dot. It's a vertical section. The details of cross section are stored in historic spot. To visit historic spot can be deep immersed in the time of cross section of ancient, to appreciate custom and habit at that time, collect the remains at that time, count the footprints of ancestor, obtain wisdom crystallize of many ancestors, know the hardship of ancestor's strive, and be graceful for them in mind, think to follow up the past and usher in the future.

Let's go to visit! Nature is a big book we can't read all over and visiting have a surplus, written by Creator's wonderful pen, more abundant than any book writing with characters; scenic spot is a sampling of them. No matter of famous mountain or big river, in spite of mountain and water, in spite of flower, grass or tree, they exist all of the miraculous truths, hidden wisdom. To visit, to read carefully, we can obtain the wisdom of the nature, satisfy the thirst for knowledge of mind, smooth the wrinkles of the mind, cleanup the daze of mind.

Let's go to visit! Let's go to visit scenic spot and historic spot.

Let's go to visit! Particularly spring is come, warmth is the weather, gentle breeze blows, scene is bright and charming, hundred flowers are bloomed, sing the bird and fragrant the flower, it's just the best time for visiting. Go! Let's go to visit!

只想到溪頭

走向溪頭！

是為了避暑？為了賞景？

路向山中行。水準漸漸高起。越來越遠離平地，遠離文明，遠離塵囂。越來越接近山，接近溪頭⋯⋯

終於到了，在爬坡、爬坡又爬坡後。

眼前是綠樹，綠樹呀綠樹、綠樹、綠樹⋯⋯

綠樹，撒下無數濃蔭，無數清涼。

沿著步道行⋯⋯。

步道，不管鋪了柏油的，未鋪柏油的，鋪了石級的，未鋪石級的，大多小小的。

所有的指路牌，都用木頭。原始呀！

那是幽篁。那是南洋杉。那是大學池。那是櫻花。那是神木。那是活動中心。那是銀杏。那是水鹿。那是苗圃。那是孔雀園。那是雜草灌木。那是諸花。⋯⋯

走在步道上。走在花旁。走在樹林間。⋯⋯

風輕輕吹送著，吹送來鳥唱、蟲鳴、草香、木香、花香和土香⋯⋯

風輕輕吹送著，吹送來靜謐、清涼、撫慰、舒適、平和和愉悅⋯⋯

沿著步道而行，去看花、草、樹木，看山，看風景，看大自然這本大書所寫的許多奧祕⋯⋯

走向溪頭！

是為了避暑？為了賞景？

不要問！我只想到溪頭。

I just Want to Xitou

Go to Xitou!

For rid of summer hot? Or for enjoy scenery?

The road marches to the mountain. The level rises slowly. It's more and more far from flat ground, far from civilization, far from mortal world. More and more near mountain, near Xitou…

At last it's arrived, after climb and climb and climb again.

Right my eyes are the green trees, wow, the green trees green trees and green trees…

The green trees sprinkle the thick shadow limitless, cool limitless.

Walk alone the pathway…

In spite of it posts asphalt or not, is it post stone step or not, the path almost small.

Whole the signpost is made by log. For it's primary!

That is bamboo. That is araucaria cunninghamii. That is university pond. That is oriental cherry. That is god tree. That is gingko. That is sambar deer. That is nursery. That is peacock field. Those are weeds and bushes. Those are flowers…

Walk on the pathway. Walk by the flower. Walk among the forest…

Wind blows slightly, brings the soing of bird, the chirp of insect, the fragrance of grass, the sweet of tree, as well as flower and soil…

Wind blows slightly, brings the calm, cool, console, comfortable, peace and happy…

Walk alone the pathway, to visit the flower, grass, tree, to visit the mountain, to visit scenery, to visit the secret written by the great book of nature…

Go to Xitou!

For rid of summer hot? Or for enjoy scene?

Don't ask me! I just want to Xitou.

秋的腳印

秋來了。

秋到處遊走著，像一個灑脫的俠客，像一個流浪者，像一個醉漢，衣履寬鬆，絲帶飄逸，行止不羈，邊走邊喃喃自語……。

秋的腳步是細碎而凌亂的。只要秋到人間，到處便有她細碎凌亂的腳印。

葉子被踩了。腳印紛紛留在葉子上。葉子曾經是青蔥、蒼翠、肥碩的，現在被踩得趨向黃澄、細瘦、枯凋了。當然，秋的腳印也踩出繽紛的顏彩。楓葉便是最好的例子。它們的反應那麼靈敏，一夜之間，便狂燃起紅火。

花呢？花自飄零。那些美顏、紛繁、豐腴、自得、嬌笑，被踩得紛紛成為新近的記憶，悽然的悵惘。啊，失色吧！消瘦吧！還有什麼好說的呢？果實那一陣豐滿、飽熟、碩大、香甜、令人垂涎的日子，則漸漸被踩碎踩爛了。

本來有雨的餵飼，長得肥胖的溪流，這下被踩得漸次枯瘦，準備到冬日裡去休息，掛著一臉蒼白、畏縮、委頓、顫抖。

鳴唱的蟲鳥也被踩得由興奮的巔峰，開始懶懶地下坡了；太陽也被踩得不那麼暴烈，開始和顏悅色了……。

秋就是這樣遊走著，邊走邊喃喃自語，像一個灑脫的俠客，像一個流浪者，像一個醉漢，腳步細碎而凌亂，留下細碎凌亂的腳印……。

The footprints of the Autumn

Autumn is here.

Autumn strolls everywhere, likes a free and easy chivalrous expert swordsman, likes a wanderer, likes a drunkard, loose in his dress and shoe, smudges in his silk and belt, frees from restraint in his action, murmurs himself while walking...

The steps of autumn are fine and in a mess. Only autumn comes, there are her fine and mess footprints everywhere.

The leaves were treaded. There were all sorts of footprints on leaves. The leaves once dark green, verdant, fat and bulky, and now are treaded into golden, weak and thin, withered. Of course, footprints of autumn are also treaded colours in riotous. Maple leaves are the best sample. Their reactions are so sensitive, wild burn into red fire in a night.

What about the flower? Flower is faded and fallen itself. The beautiful face, numerous and complicated, splendid, self-satisfied, tender laugh were treaded into all sorts of new memory, desolate disappointed and perplexed. Alas, let it be eclipsed! Become thin! What has anything to say? In fact, the days of fruit in full, plum, large, sweet, mouthwatering is treaded into break and worn-out.

Originally, there is nursed by rain, the full river, now it's treaded into wither and thin, intent to rest in the winter, hangs a face of pale, shrink, decline, shiver.

The singing bird and insect are treaded downhill into lazy slowly also; the sun is treaded into not so violent also, starts to appear with amiable looks...

Then autumn strolls, murmurs self while walking, likes a free and easy chivalrous expert swordsman, likes a wanderer, likes a drunkard, the steps are small and fragmentary, remains the small and fragmentary footprints...

秋海棠

遙遠的東方有一條江，
它的名字就叫長江；
遙遠的東方有一條河，
它的名字就叫黃河。
……

是有那麼一葉秋海棠呀，定靜地展現在花園中，那花園中的秋海棠的植株上，在那遙遠的東方，那古老的東方，那現時的東方。

一葉秋海棠，葉肉平鋪，葉脈縱橫，那是什麼徵象？具有什麼奧義？

確然，那平鋪的葉肉是平原，是高原，是三角洲，是盆地，是沙漠。不是嗎？那不是黃淮平原？松遼平原？……那不是長江三角洲？珠江三角洲？……那不是黃土高原？青藏高原？……那不是四川盆地？吐魯番盆地？……那不是戈壁大沙漠？……

確然，那縱橫的莖脈是河流，是山嶽。不是嗎？那不是長江？黃河？鴨綠江？漢水？淮河？……那不是喜瑪拉雅山？五嶽？太行山？……

還有，那湖泊？那丘陵？……那可不也是點綴那秋海棠的風景？將這秋海棠點綴得更美？

只可惜，這頁秋海棠，卻沉陷在記憶中，在夢裡，在無盡的懷思中……。

The Begonia

There is a river in the far east,
Its name is called Yangtze river;
There is a river in the far east,
Its name is called Huanghe.
… …

There is a leave of the begonia, unfolds in the garden calmly, on the plant of the begonia in the garden, in the far east, in the ancient east, in the existing east.

A leave of the begonia, even spreads the pulp, in length and breadth the vein, what is it symbolized? What does profound meaning is it?

Certainly, the pulp plane even spreads is the plane, the plateau, the triangle delta, the basin, the desert. Is it not? Is it not the huáng huái píng yuán, the sōng liáo píng yuán?… Is it not the Yangtze triangle delta? The pearl river triangle delta?… Is it not the Loess Plateau, the Tibetan Plateau?… Is it not the Sichuan Basin, the Turfan basin?… Is it not the Gobi the great Desert?…

Certainly, the length and breadth of the vein are the rivers, the mountains. Is it not? Is it not the Yangtze River? Not the Yellow River? Not the Yalu River? Not the Hanshui? Not the Huailhe River?… Is it not The Himalayes? Not the Five Sacred Mountains? Not the Taihang Mountains?…

Besides, the lake? The hills?… Is it not the landscape to decorate the begonia? To decorate begonia into more beautiful?

Only it's unfortunately, this leave of the begonia is immersed in the memory, in the dream, in the missing ceaseless…

秋葉

時序已入秋了。秋風一吹，草木的葉子，紛紛變了顏色，有的掉落地上……。

這是秋葉。

從秋葉裡，可以撫觸生命成長的痕跡，嗅聞生命成熟的甜香，窺見生命凋萎的景象。

生命的成長，一步一個腳痕，足跡斑斑。其過程是艱辛？是甜美？如人飲水，冷暖自知。許是艱辛的，許是甜美的，因人因物而異。也可能是有艱辛有甜美。艱辛和甜美相互參雜混同。艱辛總是痛苦的，萎靡的，瘦弱的；甜美時則是快樂的，蓬勃的，碩壯的，不管是艱辛是甜美，生命總在成長中趨向成熟。除非夭折；否則，當其成熟，一切便是甜美的，香醇的，令人欣喜不置。只是，生命遞嬗，循環不止，有生有死，有興有衰。生註定必趨向死。興註定必趨向衰。成熟過後，凋萎的景象是必然出現的。

這是宇宙萬物必循的定理。凡有生之物，不論壽命多長多短，誰也逃不過這個命定的必然結果，拗不過這化育的律則。

秋葉便是一個典型。它以滿臉的滑潤與皺紋述說著生命的成長、成熟，並預示著凋萎。

不要只撫觸生命成長的痕跡，耽嗅生命成熟的甜香，要珍惜現在，在冬冷來臨前，揮發自己！

The Autumn leave

The season is turned into autumn. As soon as the autumn wind blows, all sorts of leaves change their colours, some were wither and some will fall onto the earth…

This is the autumn leave.

From the autumn leave, we can touch marks the growing of life, smell the sweet mature of life, watch the scene the whither of life.

The growing of life, a step is a footprint, full of stains the footprints. The course is hardships? Or is it sweet? Only the man drinking the water knows whether it is cold or warm. May be hardships, may be sweet, it belongs to what person or thing. It also may be hardships may be sweet. Hardships and sweet mix with each other. Hardships are pain, dispirited, thin; sweet is happy, vigorous, magnificent, no matter hardships or sweet, life always tends to mature on the way of growing. Except die young; otherwise, when mature, all is sweet, fragrant and sweet, make us pleasure limitless. Only, life deliver, circles ceaselessly, will die as born, will whither as rise. Born doomed tend to be die. Rise doomed tend to be whither. Whither must be appeared after mature.

This is the theorem all things in the universe must follow. In spite of how long or short, all things alive, no one can escape this destined result bound to, difficult to break this law of growing and changing.

Autumn leave is more the model. It states the growing and mature of life with full face lubrication and wrinkle, forecast the withered.

Don't only touch marks the growing of life, indulge in smell the sweet the mature of life, must treasure now, before the coming of winter cold, volatilize yourself!

好，很好

「好，很好！」

人的心，是一切的主宰。要好，要壞，都由它。再壞的事，如果心裡認為是好的，它就會慢慢變成好的。無論遇到什麼事，再苦惱，再悲傷，再晦暗，我們的心裡都應該往好的方面想，常時在心裡說著：

「好，很好！」

管它天氣是陰雨連綿或陽光普照，早晨起床，千萬不要皺眉不快，千萬要樂觀欣喜，要常時說著：「好，很好！」這一天便會很好。本來每天都會很好嘛！之所以會不好，都是由人自招的呀！

遇到了人，不管他是年老、年輕、年少或年幼，是凶惡或良善，是識或不識，心裡要常時說著：「好，很好！」笑一笑，點點頭，一個招呼，即使是仇人，都會變得和藹可親。

吃東西的時候，不必去挑剔這個好，那個不好，心裡要常時說著：「好，很好！」那麼，所有食物，吃起來，便會甜的好，鹹的好，苦的也好。

遇倒不如意事，如以這種態度泰然處之，那麼，不如意事，其奈我何？說吧！「塞翁失馬，焉知非福？」說吧！困難是激發一個人努力向上，衝向成功的激素！心裡要常時說著：

「好，很好！」

Well, very Well

"Well, very well!"

The mind is the dominator of all things. Well or bad, up to it. The thing the worst, if the mind thinks it well, it will become well slowly. In spite of anything, if it's most trouble, most lament, most obscure, we ought to think in the well side, often to state in mind:

"Well, very well!"

No matter what the weather is cloudy and rainy a long spell of wet weather, get up in the morning, be sure don't to knit your brows, be sure to pleasure with optimistic, must often states: "Well, very well!" This day must be very well. Originally, all days will be very well! It's attracted by self if it's not well!

When meet a person, in spite of he is age, young, early young or childhood, is fierce or kind, recognized or not, we must often state in our mind: "Well, very well!" Give a smile, a nod, a call, he will be kindly even he is your enemy.

When you eat something, don't to pick on them of well or no well, we must often state in our mind: "Well, very well!" Then, all the things you eat will be the sweet is well, the salty is well, bitter also is well.

Take things calmly to the things have not gone very smoothly, then, the things have not gone very smoothly can do anything to me? Oh, state! "Misfortune may be an actual blessing?" oh, state! Difficult is a hormone to inspire a person to strive for progress and rush to success! We must often state in our mind:

"Well, very well!"

前進，繼續前進

前進，繼續前進，不要停止！

前進，繼續前進，堅持到底！

事無難易，只要前進，繼續前進，就能成功；如果中途停止，就功虧一簣了。

事情容易時，最怕意志鬆懈；如果這樣，就會像童話龜兔賽跑中的兔子，無所逃於失敗的命運。不要這樣！要前進，繼續前進，才能成功。

事情如果是困難的，更要堅定信心，堅強意志，前進，繼續前進，務求底於成功。

人在濃霧中行走，只見眼前一片茫茫，沒有底處；但是，只要不退縮，不畏懼，邁開腳步，前進，繼續前進，霧便自然散開讓路。人生前途不也如此？茫茫一片，誰能預知？但是，只要不怕苦，不怕難，邁開腳步，前進，繼續前進，前途必然開朗。

哥倫布在茫茫大海中航行，乘風破浪，夜以繼日，憑藉的是什麼？他所憑藉的只是前進的意志，前進，繼續前進，終於發現了新大陸。

前進！進得一寸是一寸。進得一尺是一尺。……

超越過去！超越自己！超越現狀！前進！再前進！繼續前進！

前進，繼續前進，不要停止！

前進，繼續前進，堅持到底！

Go Forward

Go forward. Go forward successively. Don't stop!

Go forward. Go forward successively. To hold on straight to the end!

Whether the thing is difficult or easy, only go forward, go forward successively, it can be success; if stop on the half way, it will fall short of completion by one basket of earth.

When the affair is easy, afraid the most is loose the determination; as thus, it will like the hare in race of the hare and the tortoise in the fairy tale, can't escape from the fate of failure. Don't do as thus! You must go forward, go forward successively and will success.

If the affair is difficult, you must affirm your self-confident, strong your determination, go forward, go forward successively, it's sure to be success.

When go among the fog, a person only meets a piece of foggy scene infront of him, no know of the termination; however, only don't shrink back, don't to be afraid, step forward, go forward, go forward successively, the fog will naturally disperse and give way. Isn't it so the future? It's a piece of foggy, who can predict? However, only don't to be afraid of bitter, don't to be afraid of difficulty, step forward, step forward, go forward, go forward successively, the future must be clear.

Christopher Columbus sailed on the foggy ocean, braved winds and waves, day and night, what is he relied on? He only relied on the determination of go forward, go forward, go forward successively, he discovered the New World at the end.

Go forward! An inch is an inch. A chi is a chi...

Surpass the pass. Surpass self. Surpass present situation. Go forward! Go forward again! Go forward successively!

Go forward. Go forward successively. Don't stop!

Go forward. Go forward successively. To hold on straight to the end!

鳥

　　鳥，大自然的舞蹈家，大自然的歌唱家，人類智慧的啟發者，人類心靈的安慰者。

　　鳥，是大自然的舞蹈家。只要不是睡著，牠們便無時無刻都在舞蹈著，展現美妙舞姿：翩翩飛翔是最好的美姿了，或一衝直上青天，急飛馳翔，或展翅停空、盤旋、滑行，或俯衝而下。此外，牠們一停立，一舉頭，一俯視，一跳躍，一彎身，一振翅，一洗羽，一翹尾……也都是很好的舞姿。牠們本來就身材玲瓏精緻，動作伶俐巧妙！

　　鳥，是大自然的歌唱家。牠們時常不停地唱著歌：吱吱喳喳，喞喞啾啾，咕咕嚕嚕，嗚嗚嘰嘰，咿咿呀呀……。牠們唱著，或獨唱，或合唱，或輪唱，或高或低，或抑或揚，或疾或徐，或長或短，或大或小，依其需要，該停便停，該唱便唱，融成天籟，渾然天成，悅人聽聞。

　　鳥，人類智慧的啟發者。牠們啟發了人類的智慧，尤其啟發他們發明飛行物，研發出各種舞蹈，也學著牠們創作譜曲，運用樂器或自己的發聲器，發出優美的歌唱。

　　鳥，是人類心靈的安慰者。這是最重要的。鳥，不管是舞蹈，是歌唱，是停立，都是美的，善的，除啟發人類的智慧而外，更予人類心靈以安慰，使人類心平氣和、寧謐、安詳、有歸宿。

　　是的，鳥是大自然的舞蹈家，大自然的歌唱家，人類智慧的啟發者，人類心靈的安慰者。

　　我讚美鳥！我歌頌鳥！

Birds

Birds, they are the dancers of the nature, the singers of the nature, the inspirers of the wisdom of human beings, the comforters of the soul of human beings.

Birds are the dancers of the nature. Only they aren't in sleeping, they are dancing every hour and moment, unfold their pretty dancer's posture and movement: the best postures are flied flutter, may onto sky in a rush, flies quickly, may spread their wings stay in the sky, circle, glide, may dive down. Besides, they stand, raise their heads, look down, jump, bent their body, shake their wings, wash their feathers, get cocky... are also pretty posture. They have exquisite bodies originally, they have the cleaver movement!

Birds are the singers of the nature. They often sing ceaselessly: chatter-chatter, squeak and chirp, coo-coo, creak-creak, guo-guo... they sing, some are high, some are low, some are long, some are short, some are in succession, some are off and on, may strong, may soft, may solo, may chorus, may sing in unison, may round, according to meet the demand, stop while ought to stop, sing while ought to sing, blend into sounds of nature, constitute naturally, pleasant to the ear.

Birds are the inspirers of the human beings. They inspire the wisdom of human beings, especially they inspire them to invent aircraft, research and produce every kind of dance, and also learn from them to set to music, use the musical instruments or speaking valves, to send off beautiful songs.

Birds are the comforters of the soul of human beings. This is the most important thing. In spite of dance, in spite of sing or stand, birds are pretty, kind, except for inspire wisdom of human beings, they more comfort the soul of human beings, make human beings in peace, tranquil, fit and fine, have a final state.

Yes, birds are the dancers of the nature, the singers of the nature, the inspirers of the wisdom of human beings, the comforters of the soul of human beings.

I praise bords! I eulogize birds!

雲海

　　我看過雲海，一次，再一次，在那些高山上，在多次飛行中，在多水氣的季節，至今印象深刻，銘記不忘，每次想起，便歷歷在目。

　　雲海，雲組成的海！

　　雲海，好神奇的海！

　　雲海，多變幻的海！

　　是海呀！它有多廣？多深？誰知道！聽不到澎湃聲，卻可看見波濤。它們或奔流，激起白浪花，如牧野群羊，令人心動，神馳；或洶湧，掀起高樓般巨浪，如龍似虎，令人駭怕，悚慄；或微漾，深而且藍，如靜靜處女，令人深思，喜愛。

　　有島嶼散置其間，或大或小，神祕非常。那是未被「淹沒」的山頭。至於島上有否珍寶儲藏？有否漁人被漂流到這裡，與野人打鬥，掙扎求生，過魯賓遜似的生活？有否仙人奇妙的故事？……那就只好訴諸各人去馳騁他的想像了。

　　是的。那是個任人馳騁想像的地方。可以想像到八荒九垓，可以想像到有魚龍群游海中，有海底奇景，可以想像到漁人的豐收，老船長的故事，可以想像到風景和海嘯，神仙和惡魔……。

　　雲海，雲組成的海，好神奇的海，多變幻的海，它常時留存在我心中，銘記不忘！

Sea of clouds

I have seen sea of clouds, one time, and next time, on the mountain, on fly many times, at water vapour season, are impressed on me until now, bear firmly in my mind and never forget, clearly in my mind while think of it every time.

Sea of clouds, the sea composed by clouds!
Sea of clouds, what a magic sea!
Sea of clouds, what a changeful sea!

It's surely the sea! How wide is it? How deep is it? Who knows it! We can't hear the sound of its surging, but can see the breakers. They may rush on in a torrent, stir the white spray, like group of goats on the pasture, makes us gallop in our mind; or may raging, raise big spray tower like building, like dragon as tiger, makes us fear and horrified; or may slight overflow, dark blue, like silent maiden, makes us think deeply about, love it.

There are islands spread among them. They may be big or small, very mystical. Those are the hilltops no drown. As to, it is stored the treasure, is the fisherman drifted there, fight with the barbarian, struggle to live on, live as Robinson? Is there the wonderful story of the fairy?... It just relies on everyone to gallop his imagination.

Yes. it's a place for everyone to gallop his imagination. We may imagine any place of the earth, we may imagine of the wonderful sight in the bottom of the sea the group of fishes and dragons swimming, we may image the bumper harvest of the fisherman, the stories of the old skippers, we may imagine landscape and tsunami, fairy and demon...

Sea of clouds, the sea composed by clouds, the magic sea, the changeful sea, it often lingering in my mind and never forget!

菟絲花

　　名稱只是一個符號。不管稱她菟絲子這個本名，稱她豆寄生、吐血絲、無根草、菟絲、菟蘆、菟縷、絲子、金絲草、天碧草、無根葛等等別名，對她都沒什麼影響。只要認定了對象，她便全力以赴，毫無條件地，全心全意地，愛，即使犧牲自己生命，仍然至死不渝。

　　緊擁著，緊抱著，緊纏著，緊繞著，

　　擁之抱之不足，繼之以纏，以繞，

　　傾出全部的愛，授之以全生命，絲絲縷縷，

　　莖蔓不足，繼之以吸根的千手，

　　緊擁再緊擁，緊抱再緊抱，緊纏再緊纏，緊繞再緊繞……

　　用力！用力！再用力！

　　竭盡了氣力，連本根都拋棄了，仍然奮不顧身，

　　終於全身都細瘦了，臉色蒼黃了。

　　唉。是註定了的。

　　總之，全豁出去了：至死不渝！

　　無怨！無悔！是心甘情願的，是全心全意的，是毫無條件的，有什麼好說的？

　　多動人心魄的愛情故事！相信沒有人不會被深深感動的！這可不是偉大兩個字所能畢其功竟其事的！

　　外表看起來，她是柔弱的；但她果真是柔弱的？不是的！她有愛，堅貞不移，已十分完美、堅強，一無缺憾！

The Dodder

Name is just a symbol. In spite of call it in the original name, or byname as goldthread, cuscuta chinesis etc. is not any influence to it. Only holds the target, she will do her best with all out, to love, with not any condition at all, wholeheartedly, even give up her life, never stop till death.

Hugs tightly, embraces tightly, lingers tightly, tangles tightly,

No enough of hug and embrace, follows with linger, tangle,

Exhausts whole the love, imparts whole the life, continually,

No enough of the stem and vine, follows with thousands of suck roots,.

Hugs tightly and embraces tightly again, lingers tightly and tangles tightly again,

Put forth self! Put forth self! Pay forth self again!

Exhausts the force, even former roots is cast, to dash on bravely with no thought of personal safety still

Eventually, whole the body is thin, face is fade.

Alas. It's the destiny

Above all, all is offered: never stop till death!

No regret! No repent! It is willingly and gladly, but wholeheartedly, no any condition, what words can you say?

What a story to move and thrill others? It is believed that no anyone will not moved deeply by it! This isn't the word mighty can accomplish the whole task at one strike!

She is weak at the appearance; but is she true weak? No! She has love, unswerving, very perfect, sturdiness, no any defection!

紙船

看見紙船了，在雨中。

有幾個孩子在放紙船，呼叫笑鬧著，淋得一身濕。

「我的紙船速度好快嘛！」

「我的才快呢！快！快！……你看，追過你的了！我的贏了。」

「等著瞧吧！下一次我一定要贏回來！」

其實，我寧願說，這是在夢中。夢中也下雨了。雨像斷了線的真珠，一顆顆被灑開來，灑出清涼。水溝裡的水，漲高漲大了，把水溝漲成了長江大河。是的，是雨，也是夢，給漲成的。紙船在其中乘風破浪，成為海上巨鯨。這樣不會沉沒？不會！就是不會！夢把它們幻成了木造鐵製的大船了。夢把它們托住了。不是吹的？不是！是夢！夢的力量好大！可以把無變為有，把壞變為好，把弱變為強。

夢的力量好大！它不僅把小水溝漲成了長江大河，汪洋大海，把紙船幻化成了木造鐵製的大船，把無變有，把小變大，把壞變好，把弱變強，還把船上加了填充物。船是滿載了的。滿載著什麼？是理想！是愉悅！航抵目的地是理想。呼叫笑鬧是愉悅的表現。船乃載著滿滿的理想和愉悅前航，光輝燦爛，令人無限讚嘆……。

還是在下雨。還是在夢中。有幾個孩子在放紙船，呼叫笑鬧著，淋得一身濕……。

The Paper Boat

I view the paper boat, in the rain.

There are some children sail the paper boat, calling, hailing, laughing and noising, whole their bodies are drenched with rain.

"How quick the speed of my paper boat!"

"It's quick of mine! Quickly! Quickly!... Lo, it pursues ahead yours! Mine is won!"

"You may see! I'll win next time!"

In fact, I prefer to say this is in the dream. It's rained in the dream also. The rain likes the pearls broke off the strings, spreads one grain after another, sprinkles the cool. The water in the ditch rises into high and fully, rising the ditch into large river. Yes, it's the rain and the dream also, rising it. Paper boat braves winds and waves in it, and becomes illusorily, to be big whale. Can't it sink? No. It just can't. This is the dream let them into big boats made by iron and wood. Dream supports them. Isn't it a boast? No. It's the dream. How large the power of dream! It can change nothing to be something, change bad into good, weak to be strong.

How large the power of dream! It doesn't only rise the small ditch into large river, into boundless body of water, change illusorily paper boat into big boats made by iron and wood, change nothing to be something, change small into large, change bad into good, weak to be strong, even more add stuffs illusorily onto the boat. The boat is full load carry. What is it loaded fully? It's load fully with ideal! It's loaded fully with pleasure! Sail to terminate is the ideal. Calling, hailing, laughing and noising is the express of pleasure. Boat sail forward with loaded fully ideal and pleasure, splendously, can be struck with admiration...

It's rained still. It's in the dream still. There are some children sail the paper boat, calling, hailing, laughing and noising, whole their bodies are drenched with rain.

燭火

入夜以後，天暗了下來。

尤其是亮著的燈也突然熄了

「停電了。」

「媽！鬼來了。」

「好暗喲！」

更尤其是颱風天，風雨不但不停，而且變本加厲──一片雜亂、孤獨、茫然、徬徨、恐懼的感覺，便一把攬住了你，緊緊地，一點都不放鬆，若是冬天，便加上寒冷、顫抖……。

「別怕！我來點亮蠟燭！」

「對！把蠟燭點起來！」

一根蠟燭被點燃了。

一片光芒傳佈開來。

哇！好亮呀！

所有的雜亂、孤獨、茫然、徬徨、恐懼，甚至寒冷、顫抖，都驚逃了。

燭火在空際搖曳著。風懷著惡意，想把它吹熄。它堅持著，要燃亮！

為什麼要被吹熄？

我是燭。我要燃亮起來！我要燃燒自己，擎起光明，照亮別人！

朋友！別詛咒黑暗，要燃亮自己！

The Candle

It's getting dark after it's in the night.

It's dark especially when the lamp light is extinguished abruptly.

"The power is out."

"Ghost is coming, Mon!"

"How dark it is!"

It's darker especially in typhoon day, not only the wind and rain hasn't stop, but also more intensify--all are bogged down in the feeling of a piece of disorder, solitary, at a loss, hesitate and dread will grasp you, tightly, doesn't loosen a little, and will add chill and tremble if it's in winter...

"Don't be afraid of it! Let me ignite a candle!"

"Yes. Ignite the candle!"

A candle is ignited.

A ray of light is spread.

Wow, how bright it is!

All the disorder, solitary, at a loss, hesitate and dread are escaped with hurry, even the chill and tremble.

The candle swings in the air. Wind may extinguish it with vicious intent, but it persists in bright!

Why it's to be extinguished?

I'm a candle. I want to burn bright! I want to burn self, hold the bright, lighting others.

My dear friend, don't curse dark, you must brighten self!

燈

當白天依循著大自然的規律，被時間推擁著，走向命運必然的歸宿，黑暗便以其綿密的細網，遮覆住世界，使夜漆黑不堪；如果再加上無星無月，夜更是黑越越的，讓人不辨天地了。此時，燈顯得多麼重要呀！

燈和光，形如骨之與肉，只要有燈，光明便永在。

黑暗，予人一種茫然、困惑、恐懼、不祥的感覺。沒有人喜歡黑暗，也沒有人不喜歡光明。「多希望有一盞燈呀！」在黑暗中，這是人們心中的最大想望。此時，果真出現一盞燈，便有如跋涉在無盡的沙漠中，渴極欲飲，忽見綠洲甘泉，有如迷失在荒山野林中，餓極欲食，忽見飯菜，有如連續一週不眠不休，睏極欲睡，倦極欲休，忽然獲得睡覺休息的機會，有如在困頓失望中，忽然獲得一絲解決的端倪，其喜悅之情，怎可計量？

「啊，有燈了！」

「啊，光明在望了！」

路燈，佇立路旁，以其光芒為手指，指引人們回家的路，指引人們走向光明大道……。

燈塔，佇立海邊，以其閃光為訊號，指引茫茫大海中的船舶，使不致迷失，航抵目的地……。

每一個人的心中，也都要有一盞燈，引導著他，走向光明大道，錦繡前程……。

The Lamp

When day is pushed by time according to the rule of nature, walks to the inevitable termination of fate, dark will cover the world with its fine and dense net, make night to be pitch-black; if it's no moon and star, it will blacker, let us can't distinguish all things of the world. It appears that how importance is the lamp.

Lamp and light like bone and flesh, light will exist forever only there is a lamp.

Dark gives us the feeling of at a loss, bewildered, fear, unlucky. Nobody likes dark, nobody dislikes light too. "Wishing there is a lamp!" This is the biggest wishing of everybody while in the dark. If there truly appears a lamp, it will like a person trudging in the unlimited desert, extremely hoping for drink, views suddenly the oasis and spring of sweet well, like lose his way in barren mountain and wild forest, want to have food when hungry extremely, meets food suddenly, likes he no sleep and rest a week successively for a week, sleepy extremely to want to sleep, tired extremely to want to rest, obtains an opportunity to sleep and rest, likes in the lose and fatigued, obtains a little clue for solution suddenly, how to measure the pleasure?

"Oh, it is the lamp!"

"Light is hopping!"

Street lamp, stands by the roadside, points and leads everybody the road for back home, points and leads everybody to go on the bright road…

Light house, stands on sea bank, with the shining lamp, points and leads the boat on the vast sea, gets no lose, sails to termination…

In the heart of everybody, ought to have a lamp, leads him to go on brilliant road, beautiful future…

新娘花

　　新娘花，新娘的花，以新娘名花，好美的名字呀！

　　它是最受歡迎的花，尤其是現在，天氣冷了，新娘出現的頻率增加，更是備受歡迎。它總是充滿著喜氣洋洋，也帶給人們洋洋喜氣。

　　它的莖葉是那麼綠綠細細的，成羽毛狀，伸展出去，橫生出去，鋪陳出去，細細碎碎地織成一面細網，予人許多聯想：

　　——這是一張愛情之網，要網住的是雙方的心。

　　——這是一片夜空，五角星形的花便是夜空中的星了，一顆顆點
　　　　綴著，遠望過去，真還一閃一閃著呢。

　　——這是青春男女的夢之所繫，很羅曼蒂克味的。他們奮不顧身
　　　　地投入，為它所纏繞，也互相纏繞。

　　嗯，想起來了。這是獨一無二的花。這是任何花都無可倫比的花。

　　是了，新娘花是獨一無二、無可倫比的花。在婚禮上捧著的那雙手，更必然是獨一無二、無可倫比的手。看！那麼細緻、柔滑、稚嫩而豐滿，那麼神奇，富於夢幻，是創造喜悅、美滿和幸福的手！人世間到哪裡去找這樣的一雙手？

　　哦，就讓這一雙手捧著新娘花，在一片洋洋喜氣間，捧出一個羅曼蒂克的愛情之夢，捧出喜悅、美滿和幸福吧！

The Blushing bride

The blushing bride, the flower for the bride, named the flower with bride, how great is the name!

It's the flower be welcomed the most, especially right now, the weather is cold, the frequency range the bride appear is increase, it's more be welcomed. It always beaming with joy, and also brings beaming with joy to people.

It's green and fine in the stem and leaf, feather-like in shape, stretches out, grows wild out, spreads out, fine and closely woven into the net, makes us to associate with:

–This is a piece of love net, wants to trap the hearts of both sides.

–This is a piece of night sky, the five angles star shape flower is the star in the night sky, decorates one after another, and still sprinkles truly look from far away.

–This is the tie the dream of the youth, very romantic. They cast them regardless of their safety, tangled by them, and also tangle with each other.

Oh, I see. It's the unique flower. It's the incomparable flower.

Yes, the blushing bride is the flower of unique and incomparable. The hands hold the flower is certainly the hand unique and incomparable. Lo! How tender, soft, delicate and plump the hands, how magic, dreamy the hands, are the hands to create joy, plump and happy! Where can we find this pair of hands around the world?

Oh, let this pair of hands to hold the blushing bride, in beaming with joy to people, hold the dream of love of romantic, hold joy, plump and happy!

忍冬花

　　忍耐著，堅強忍耐著，咬緊牙關地忍耐著⋯⋯。

　　忍耐著，要忍耐多久？要有多少堅強的忍耐力？

　　忍冬花，那麼細瘦，那麼嬌小，那麼纖柔，那麼金枝玉葉，被稱為金針花，能夠忍耐得起嗎？

　　冬是暴君，是惡魔，天生具有暴力傾向、虐待狂，總露出猙獰的面目，以風霜雨雪為武器，到處奔逐，到處橫行，發出呼呼碰碰聲，欺壓萬物，要令萬物蕭條，百花凋落，萬葉枯萎⋯⋯。

　　再細瘦，再嬌小，再纖細，再金枝玉葉，被稱金針花，她還是得忍耐，並且忍耐得起！

　　誰說忍耐不起？

　　他一定忍耐得起的！身上留有淚的酸味，他還是會堅強地忍耐下去，而且忍耐得起。

　　忍冬，忍冬，忍冬，忍過冬天以後。

　　忍過冬天以後，當然就是春天了。會是怎樣？

　　是的，忍過冬天以後，春天一到，便會復甦、滋長、蓬勃、開花⋯⋯。

　　只是，現在仍是冬天，她仍需忍耐：

　　再細瘦，再嬌小，再纖弱，再金枝玉葉，既然在冬天裡，就需忍耐，堅強地忍耐，咬緊牙關地忍耐⋯⋯。

　　再細瘦，再嬌小，再纖弱，再金枝玉葉，既然在冬天裡，就需忍耐，再久也需忍耐，再苦也需忍耐⋯⋯。

The Honeysuckle

Bears, bears firmly, grit teeth to bear…

Bears, how long will she bear? How much is the strong bear force need?

Honeysuckle, thin likes that, tiny likes that, slander likes that, "He's a woman, she is a man" likes that, since it's called honeysuckle, can it be bearable?

Winter is a tyrant, is a devil, posted the incline of violence inborn, mad in ill-treatment, often shows the ferocious face, arms with wind, frost, rain and snow, goes around everywhere, runs amuck everywhere, issues the sound of whir and boom, bullies all the thing, will make all the thing desolate, all the flower fall, all the leave wither…

What is more thin, more tiny, more slander, more "He's a woman, she is a man", who is called honeysuckle, she must bear, and to be bear!

Who says she can't bear?

She certainly bearable! Even after it passed, the sour tears left, she will bear firmly still, and will bearable.

Bear the winter, bear the winter, what will she be after borne the winter?

After the winter is passed, it of course is spring.

Yes, bears after winter, when spring arrived, recovery , growing, vigor, bloom will be come…

Only it's still winter, she must bear:

What is more thin, more tiny, more slander, more "He's a woman, she is a man", since it's winter, she must bear, bear firmly, grit teeth to bear…

Only it's still winter, she must bear: What is more thin, more tiny, more slander, more "He's a woman, she is a man", since it's winter, she must bear, how long it need also to bear, how hard it need to bear…

冬夜裡

當季節裡的春夏秋相繼悄然飄逸，冬季出現，時光又無聲無息地帶走白日，帶來夜晚，冬夜於是誕生，寒冷便跟著從北地遷移而來，加上斜風細雨助紂為虐的結果，寒冷便步步高升，黑暗便逐漸加深……。

當然，它也帶來顫抖、呆板、驚怕、悽楚、沉鬱、雞皮疙瘩……。

彷彿來了妖魔鬼怪，青面獠牙的……。

彷彿來了凶禽猛獸，張牙舞爪的……。

彷彿落入了一個陰森的無人之境……。

彷彿落入了一個無助的逼窄狹谷……。

彷彿有聲音在呼喊：

「多麼需要溫暖！」

「多麼需要光明！」

「但願冬天趕快過去，春天趕快來臨！」

「但願夜晚趕快過去，黎明趕快來臨！」

「但願寒冷趕快過去，溫暖趕快來臨！」

「但願黑暗趕快過去，光明趕快來臨！」

只是冬天仍在，夜晚仍在，寒冷仍在，黑暗仍在。沒關係！很快就會過去的。冬天過了春天便來。夜晚過了黎明便來。寒冷過了溫暖便來。黑暗過了光明便來。……

In the Winter Night

When spring, summer and autumn of the seasons floated away silently, winter appeared, and time also carried day away without any sound, brought the night, the winter night thence arrives, chill will follow them moves from the north, moreover, for the result of maltreats by slanting wind and drizzle, chill will rise step by step, dark will deeper slowly...

Of course, it also brings shiver, stiff, dumbness, dread, misery, depression, gooseskin...

As if it appears the evil spirits, green-face and long-toothed...

As if it appears the fierce birds and beasts, bare fangs and brandish claws...

As if it falls into a funereal place of unmanned...

As if it falls into a narrow ravine of helpless...

As if there are sounds call:

"How need I want warm!"

"How need I want brightness!"

"Wishing the winter passes away quickly, the spring arrives quickly!"

"Wishing the night passes away quickly, dawn arrives quickly!"

"Wishing the chill passes away quickly, the warm arrives quickly!"

"Wishing the dark passes away quickly, the brightness arrives quickly!"

Only winter is here still, night is here still, chill is here still, dark is here still. Never mind! It will pass very soon. Spring will come here after winter passed. Dawn will come here after night passed. Warm will come here after chill passed. Brightness will come here after dark passed...

攀登

　　攀登上去！攀登到最高處！

　　攀登上去！任它山有多高多峻多險、路有多狹窄多崎嶇多難行，即使再加上天候的惡劣——是寒冷透骨、風雨交加或烈日曝曬，都不能阻擋一個人向上的意志。堅強的意志可以克服一切艱難險阻。只要一意向上！只要一意向上！一步有一步的進境。積小步可以成為大步。「雖覆一簣，進，吾進矣！」

　　從清晨太陽的冉冉升起，可以看見攀登的影像；從火苗的漸次旺燃起來，也可以看見攀登的影像；此外，可以看見攀登的影像的，還有動物、植物的漸次長大，小孩子身心的漸次成熟，讀書人研究的漸見成績，運動員能量的漸次增進，修道者工夫的漸次增加……。

　　是的，太陽的冉冉升起詮釋著攀登的意義，火苗的漸次旺燃起來也是的，還有，動物、植物的漸次長大，小孩子身心的漸次成熟，讀書人研究的漸見成績，運動員能量的漸次增進，修道者工夫的漸次增加……。

　　攀登上去！攀登是一件大事。要摒除一切雜念的羈絆，全身投入，全心投入，集中精神，專注定力，不稍鬆懈，即使汗流浹背，受傷流血，疼痛不已，也要全力攀登。需要勉力為之，不可放棄。所有成功都需孜孜不倦，堅持努力，忍苦耐勞。

　　攀登上去！攀登向最高處！

Climb up

Climb up! Climb up to the highest!

Climb up! In spite of how high, loft, and dangerous the mountain, how narrow, rough and hard to walk the road, even adds fierce of the weather-the cold stings the bone, rains cat and dog, or in the scorching sun, can't block the intension of a person to go upward. Strong intention can conquer all the difficulty and danger. Only upward in disregard of any disturb! Only upward in disregard of any disturb! There is a progress one step and one step. Small step can accumulate into big step. "Progress, I progress though it's only a qui of soil."

We can view the image of climb up from the dawn sun rising slowly; also can view the image of climb up from the flame burn into flourishing slowly; besides, we can view still the image of the climb up from the growing slowly of the animal and plant, the ripe slowly of the mind and body of the child, the study achievement of the scholar slowly, the energy of the sportsman rising slowly, the skill of the man cultivate himself in according with a religious doctrine increasing slowly...

Yes, the rising slowly of the sun explains the meaning of climb up, it's also the flame burn into flourishing slowly, besides, the growing slowly of the animal and plant, the ripe slowly of the mind and body of the child, the study achievement of the scholar slowly, the energy of the sportsman rising slowly, the skill of the man cultivate himself in according with a religious doctrine increasing slowly...

Climb up! Climb up is a great event. Must get rid of all the fetters of miscellaneous thoughts, put in whole body, put in whole heart, concentrate whole mind, concentrate all attention, don't loose a little, even streaming with sweat, be hurt and bleed, ache extremely, also must climb up with whole heart. We must manage with an effort, never give up. All the success needs diligent assiduously, insist to hard work, bear servitude and tax on energy.

Climb up! Climb up to the highest!

皺紋正義

儘管石頭多麼堅硬踏實；但是放在屋簷下，經過柔弱的雨水所集聚成的簷滴，一滴滴日長月久地滴落，都要消融或被滴穿，何況那麼柔弱的人臉呢？

人的臉真的是柔弱不堪的，禁不起時間那細碎腳步的不斷踩踏、鑽刺、錘鍊，終於變成凹凸不平，營造出許多皺紋來了。

因為那些皺紋，使人的臉上有高山，有縱谷，有大河，有大小支流。它們縱橫交錯在臉的大地上，或大或小，或粗或細，或高或低……。

哇！不得了！時間果然不得了，能把人的臉上造得這麼原始、典雅、豐富、雄偉、精良、燦美，風格不凡，令人欽仰不已……。

是的，皺紋是令人欽仰不已的，一如漆黑夜裡的燈盞，散發出永恆的光芒，吸引來大家仰視的眼光，如眾蛾之撲火……。

在皺紋裡，隱隱閃著經驗和歷練的光芒……。

在皺紋裡，隱隱閃著智慧和學識的光芒……。

在皺紋裡，隱隱閃著血汗和辛勤的光芒……。

在皺紋裡，隱隱閃著堅忍和淚水的光芒……。

那麼，就讓時間細碎的腳步來踩踏、鑽刺、錘鍊吧！它會慢慢出現高山、縱谷、大河和大小支流的，並且終於發出燦爛永恆的光芒！

The True Meaning of Wrinkle

In spite of how hard the stone, if it lays under the eaves, experiences the drops gathered by the weak rain, drips a drop after a drop as long time of days and months went by, will be melted or pierced, let along the weak face of person?

The face of person is very weak, can't bear the trample underfoot, drill and prick, temper ceaselessly by the small and fragmentary footsteps of time, becomes rough eventually and builds many wrinkles.

Due to these footsteps, make the face of person high mountains, valleys, big rivers, tributaries. They arranged in a crisscross pattern on great land of the face, either big or small, either bulky or thin, either high or low...

Wow, how horrible! The time is truly horrible. It can make the face of person into such primary, elegant, abundant, magnificent, excellent, brilliant, graceful bearing, let us admire limitless...

Yes, wrinkle let us admire, likes the lamp in the darken night, sprinkles forever radiance, attracts the eye sight of us to up look, likes numerous moths flapping his wings toward fire...

It shines faintly the radiance of experience and temper within the wrinkle...

It shines faintly the radiance of wisdom and knowledge within the wrinkle...

It shines faintly the radiance of blood and sweat as well as diligence within the wrinkle...

It shines faintly the radiance of determination and tears within the wrinkle...

Then, let it tramples underfoot, drills and pricks, tempers ceaselessly by the small and fragmentary footsteps of time! It will appear slowly high mountains, valleys, big rivers, tributaries, and sprinkles eventually brilliant and forever radiance!

堅持

　　要堅持下去！要努力不懈！不要中途停下來！不要放棄工作！

　　天下沒有白吃的午餐。勝利不會從天上掉下來。成功不可能一蹴而及。機會成本雖然是經濟學上的原理，用在其他方面也是同樣行得通的。要有所獲得，必需付出代價。堅持是所付代價中最重要的。

　　堅持需要有極大的耐力，堅強的意志，不餒的信心，永遠不退縮。

　　一曝十寒顯然沒有成功的可能；遇到困難，就畏縮不前，或放棄工作，更會和成功絕緣。人生不如意事，十常八、九；如果一遇不如意事，就畏縮不前或放棄工作，不堅持到底，是不可能有所成就的，必也忍苦耐煩，乃能期其有成。

　　爬山者是最好的例子。一步一步爬上去，到很累了仍未達山巔，他如果放棄，便沒法爬到了；他一定要咬緊牙關，任汗去流，任氣去喘，甚至任血去流，一步一步爬上去，堅持到底，不中輟，乃能達成目標，爬上最高峰，成就那一趟爬山壯舉。

　　做其他任何事也像爬山，一定要堅持努力，繼續不輟，才能把事做成功。

　　拿破崙說：「成功屬於最堅忍者。」要堅持下去！要努力不懈！不要中途停下來！不要放棄工作！

Insist on

You ought to insist on! You ought to strive! Never stop half way! Don't give up the work!

There's no such thing as a free lunch on earth. The victory will not fall from the sky. Success can't reach in one step. Although opportunity cost is the principle of economics, it's validness also in other thing. Whoever must pay for his success. Insist on is the most price he will pay.

Insist on needs extreme patience, firm determination, no down heart of faith, never shrink back forever. It's apparently invalid that one day's sun and ten day's frost; life isn't a bed of rose, it will absolutely rid from success if shrink or give up when face difficulty. Life will meet you halfway if shrink or give up and not insist on to the terminate when face difficulty, it's impossible to be success, the person who exercises patience and endures pain, he will be success.

The climber of the mountain is the best example. A person who climbs one step after one step, and still not reach the top of the mountain till very tired, if he gives it up, he can not do the climbing; he must grit his teeth, let him streaming in sweat, has hardly recovered his breath, even bleed, climb one step after one step, insist on, not stop in half way, and will climb to the terminate, climb to the highest, achieve that great undertaking of mountain-climbing.

It's the same thing like mountain-climbing, be sure to insist on strive, not stop, successively, can achieve a work.

Napoleon Bonaparte said once: success belongs to the man who insists the most. You ought to insist on! You ought to strive! Never stop half way! Don't give up the work!

松

穿一身綠衣，戴一頭綠絨，松站立著，在地上，亭亭然，挺挺然，穩穩然，默默然！

日復一日，月復一月，年復一年，任時間在周邊身上穿行而過，它都如此，不改變！

時間總是會帶來陰晴霜雪，冷熱風雨，它都如此，肯定自我，堅持勁節，不受影響！

是的，它肯定自我，堅持勁節，不受影響。它的根深入泥土，吃土很深，可以固本！

是的，它肯定自我，堅持勁節，不受影響。它的幹，雖赤褐皺裂，卻粗壯筆直，不彎！

是的，它肯定自我，堅持勁節，不受影響。它的針葉，一勁地綠，永遠地綠，不變！

也有花。花單性，雌雄同株。也有果。果呈毯狀。這完全是遵行自然界化育的律則！

站立著，亭亭然，挺挺然，穩穩然，默默然。不言語；其實，它已言語。它以身言！

是的，它以身言！身體的語言最真切，最懇摯，也最具體。它不言語已見一切言語！

它以身體的語言述說著：我正大，挺直，勁節，堅貞，不屈，歷久不變，在艱彌勵！

喜歡松。經常去接近松。每次接近它，便讚賞不已，並在心中默許：願我是一棵松！

The Pine

Wears a green garment on body, and a hat on head, the pine stands on the land, erectly, stiffly, firmly, quietly!

The time passes through his body and four side, he is thus still, never change, day after day, month after month, year after year!

Time always brings the weather change of cloudy, sunny, frosted and snowy, cold, warm, wind and rain, he is still thus, affirms himself, insists moral spirit, don't to be influence!

Yes, he affirms himself, don't to be influence. His root penetrates into earth, absorbs earth deeply, can fix the roots!

Yes, he affirms himself, don't to be influence. Although bares and brown, his trunk is bough and straight, not bent!

Yes, he affirms himself, don't to be influence. His needle leaf is green totally, green forever, no change!

There is also the flower. Flower is parthenocarpy, hermaphrodite. And there is also the fruit. The fruit appears blanket-like shape. This all follows to the rule of nurture of the nature!

He stands, erectly, stiffly, firmly, quietly. He hasn't words; but in fact he has spoken. He speaks with his body!

Yes, he speaks with his body! Body word is the most true, most sincere, most concrete. He doesn't speak is appeared all of the word!

He speaks with his body word: I'm upright, stiffy, sturdy, firm, bendless, unchangeable, stronger while it's difficulty.

I like the pine. I get near to the pine very often. I praise it very much every time I near it, and promise to be a pine.

聖誕紅

造物這個園丁，說來算是極為公平無私的。他整年不停，日夜不歇，到處普施愛心與恩澤，給世界這座繁花遍植的大花園，澆水灌溉，施撒肥料，以霧露，以甘霖，以陽光……。

於是，春天有春天的花朵，夏天有夏天的花朵，秋天有秋天的花朵，冬天有冬天的花朵——各個季節有各個季節不同的花朵。

於是，聖誕紅展綻了。

它是極為鮮明突出的；因為冬天的花朵不多，它卻不畏寒冷，如期展綻——它和梅花，一紅一白，成為冬天裡兩個鮮明突出的風景。

它是極為與眾不同的；因為它的展綻，確實不同於其他許多別種的花。

時間一分一秒地過去，造物整年不停日夜不歇地澆水灌溉，施撒肥料，聖誕紅不住地吸取養分，儲蓄醞釀，生長壯大，枝幹漸次長粗長硬，盾形綠葉漸次加濃加深長肥，當冬天一來，紅葉便在枝頭展綻成花瓣，一片片向外橫伸排列，自然圍成一個圓圈，在眾多綠葉襯托下，更見其鮮紅如火，豔麗逾恒。

它們排列展綻著的是什麼？它們圍成的圓圈又象徵著什麼？……

啊，是和平，是聖善，是熱情，是溫暖……。

X'mas Flower

The gardener the Creator, is to be said he's upheld justice extremely. He gives love and favour to public whole year long, ceaselessly every day and night, grants the world this large garden flowers planted, watering, fertilizing, with fog and dew, with timely rain, with sunshine…

Therefore, there are the spring flowers in the spring, there are the summer flowers in the summer, there are the autumn flowers in the autumn, there are the winter flowers in the winter-every season has its different flower.

Therefore, X'mas flower will be blossomed.

It's sticking out extremely, because there are less flowers open in winter, but it no afraid of the cold, blossoms as usual, - it as well as the plum, red is one white is one, becomes two distinct and stick landscape in the winter.

It's very different from public, because its blossom is surely not the same of other flower.

The time passes one minute after one second, the Creator watering, fertilizing, day and night ceaselessly whole year, the X'mas flower absorbs the nurture successively, stores and brews, grower and stronger, branch and twig grows thick and sturdy slowly, shield-like green leave grows thick and strong and plump slowly, when winter is here, the red leave will open into petal on the top of the twig, lines up outward one by one, encircles to be a ring naturally, under the set off by multitudinous leaves, is more to be seen bright red as fire, gorgeous more over usual.

What is it they line up and open? What is it symbol again they circle to be a ring?

Oh, it's the peace, the sacred and kindness, the enthusiasm, and the warmth…

虎

　　說到虎，幾乎人人心裡都會為之震驚一下；如遇見了，更會驚嚇得不知所措。

　　牠是一隻龐然大物，看起來全身是勁，力大無比，無堅不摧，是造物的大傑作。

　　黑的一條，白的一條，牠的全身皮毛，就這樣黑白相間，形成有規則的條紋，是畫家的大手筆。

　　牠的四隻腳，是堅固而具有很大彈性的鋼筋，適合於追逐撲殺獵物，是經過鐵匠特意鑄造的。

　　牠的眼睛，是兩盞閃閃發光的燈，總是炯炯有神，不住探照著，是汽車的兩盞霧燈。

　　牠的牙齒，是鋼刀利劍，可以斬釘截鐵，咬斷所有最堅韌的骨和肉，是經過千錘百鍊的。

　　牠的尾巴，是武者手中的鐵棍，一揮一剪，虎虎生風，出神入化，不可一世，是設計家的巧妙設計。

　　只要牠鼻子兩邊皺出幾條皺紋，張開嘴來嘯叫，便有數萬爆竹同時爆炸的音量，炸彈炸開的威力，頓時山鳴谷應，人畜俱靡。

　　牠常時隱伏在洞穴裡，餓了便出來，在草野、山林間逡巡，尋找獵物。只要牠一出現，不管是山禽、野鳥都會噤聲不鳴，不論是山羌、野兔、山鹿、野牛、野馬、山羊，以至人類，都會逃之夭夭。

　　虎，剛強，猛武，陽性的平方物！

The Tiger

Refer to the tiger, almost everyone will take a shock in his mind; and will be frighten into not knowing how to do.

He is a huge monster, looks like he is powerful all his body, having matchless strength, capable of destroying any stronghold, is the great masterpiece of Creator.

A stripe of black, a stripe of white, all his skin of body is thus alternate with white and black, forms into regularly stripe, the great handwriting of the artist.

His four feet are the hard and elasticity reinforcing bar, fit for him to chaste and catch the prey. They casted by the blacksmith specially.

His eyes are two shining lamp, always brimming with radiating vigour, searching ceaselessly, two fog lamps of the motor vehicle.

His teeth are steel knifes and sharp swords, can resolute the nail and decisive the iron, bite the most solid and tough flesh and bone into pieces,are tempered thoroughly .

His tail is the iron stick of the knight, a wield and a wipe, marvelous vigour,of highest perfection, unchallengeable, the smart design of the designer.

Only the winkles beside his nose take some winkles, opens his mouth and roar, there are volumes of sound which exploded by ten thousands of firecrackers at the same time, the power of the bomb exploded, sounding the mountains and resounded the valleys immediately, decadent both the people and the cattle.

He often hides in the cave, and searches for the preys among the grass field and forest when he is hungry. Only he is appeared, no matter the mountain fowls or wild birds will be mute, no matter Chinese muntjac, hare, deer, buffalo, wild horse, goat, as to mankind all will escape.

The tiger, strong, fierce, square of masculine gender!

抱怨

　　人類是會抱怨的動物，而且，何止會抱怨已爾？還是很會抱怨的動物呢！

　　謂之不信，且聽我道來！

　　冬天，天氣冷了，人類就抱怨老天不好，說老天為什麼會讓天氣那麼冷？希望冷趕快過去；可是，到了夏天，天氣熱了，又抱怨老天不好了，說老天為什麼讓天氣那麼熱？都要熱死了！希望熱趕快過去。

　　同樣地，乾旱時，人類便抱怨老天不好，說老天為什麼不下雨，是不是要把人類乾旱死了？等雨季來時，多下幾天雨，他便又抱怨老天不好了，說老天為什麼不停下雨，把人困在屋裡，骨頭都要發霉了，如造成水災，那老天更不知要被罵成什麼樣子了。

　　人類抱怨這個抱怨那個，好像萬物必需皆備於我，聽我主宰；否則便不滿意，萬物有負於我，活該有罪，非給抱怨一下不可。

　　其實，人類會抱怨沒什麼不好，不但沒什麼不好，而且還有好處。

　　人類之所以抱怨，是人類天生有不滿足、求好的性格。沒有的時候要求有，有了以後要求好，好了以後要求更好，有缺點就要求改進，所謂「精益求精」就是了。人類的文化進步就是這樣來的。

　　那麼，就去抱怨吧！就去不滿吧！就去求好吧！我們將在抱怨、不滿、求好中更加精進！

Complaint

Human being is an animal who can complain, and far more than complain? He is great in complaining!

Let me tell you if you won't to believe.

The weather is cold, human being complains the heaven is no good, says why the hearen let the weather so cold? Wishing the cold will pass quickly; but when summer is come, the weather is hot, he also complains the heaven is no good, says why the heaven let the weather so hot? It's burning! Wishing the hot will pass quickly.

It's the same, when it's drought, human being will complain the heaven is not good, says why the heaven don't rain, as if drought brings human being into death. When rain season is come, as rain is drop more days, he also complains the heaven is no good, says why it's rain ceaselessly, surrounds person in the house, the bone will become mouldy, if it causes flood, the heaven will to be blamed to death.

Human being complains hither and thither, as if everything must ready for me, dominated by me, or it will be discontented, everything is fail to come up to me, it deserves the punishment, it's no choice but to complain.

In fact, human being to complain is not bad, not only not bad but also has benefit.

Why human being complained is human being has the nature of dissatisfy and forward to good. Want to have something when there is nothing, will search to good when they have something, search better when it's good, must revise when there are some shortcomings, this is so called "to always endeavor to do still better; to strive for perfection". The improving of the culture of human being is the fruit as thus.

Then, to complain! To dissatisfy! To search for good! We will get more improvement in the complaint, dissatisfy and search for good!

丟棄

在人的一生中，有許多事物是需要珍惜的；但卻有不少事物是可以丟棄的。該丟棄的事物，便要毅然丟棄，不要捨不得。捨不得可能徒然造成許多累贅。

讀書人最常為各種報紙、雜誌、字紙、書、稿等資料所苦。資料固然要儲存；但是許多人儲存了些對自己無關重要的資料或儲存時認為重要的資料，定然占了地方，以致書櫥、書桌、抽屜甚至床下、地板等等到處都是，髒亂成一團，收拾困難，束手無策。

許多人家裡常常會有許多不用的東西。許是孩子的舊玩具，許是用過的家具，買的時候，可能自覺很貴重，很美好，用很高的價格買下；但是，玩過一陣子，用過一陣子，不喜歡了，不用了，或者隨處一放，或者儲之倉庫，久而久之，忘了，任它們在那裡落滿灰塵、腐壞。

有些人有壞習慣，譬如不莊重、散漫、不專心、偷懶、吸食毒品、作奸犯科等等，這些壞習慣往往戕害他的一生，甚至危害國家、社會、人類。有這些壞習慣的人，應痛下決心，毅然丟棄，成為一個有用之人。

世上事物有該珍惜的，有該丟棄的。該珍惜的便要珍惜，該丟棄的尤其要下決心，毅然丟棄。時時檢查，時時反省，該丟棄的便予丟棄——丟棄那些舊的，不好的，不要捨不得，方能輕鬆，不受累贅。

Cast away

In our whole life, there are many things must to be treasured but there are many things can be cast away. Cast away resolutely ought to cast away, don't be unwilling to. Unwilling to cast away will cause many burdensome to no avail.

The scholar often feels trouble by the data of newspapers, magazines, wastepaper, books and manuscripts etc. Of course the data must deposit; but many people deposit no important or may important deem then, surely occupied space, so that book cases, desks, drawers even under the beds, floors etc. in everywhere, mess all around, difficult to clean, are at a loss to know what to do.

Frequently there are many useless things in many families. May be the old toys, may be the furniture, possibly they are very valuable as they deemed themselves, great beauty, bought them with very high price; but played for a short time, used for a short time, disliked it, perhaps places it anywhere, perhaps deposited it in storehouse, for a long time forgot it, let them full of dust, rotten.

May someone have bad habit, for instance, undignified, undisciplined, absentminded, idle, drug taking, crime etc., these bad habits will often do harmful to his whole life, even do harmful to country, society and human being. The people who holds these bad habits, ought to make up their mind, cast away resolutely, to be a useful person.

Things in the world, some ought to treasure, some ought to cast away. We must treasure ought to treasure, those ought to cast away must make up mind cast away resolutely. Self examination, self-reflection, cast away those ought to cast away, --cast away those old, no good, don't be unwilling to, and will be relaxed, free of burdensome.

勤勞

物以類聚。這是自古而然的，乃是造物者當初造物所訂下的律則，更是宇宙間萬物參贊化育的自然之道，不可移易。不是嗎？火就燥。水流濕。不是嗎？牛吃草。貓吃魚。至於人類，不也是一樣？醜惡總是集向壞人。榮譽總是歸諸好人。連為惡都會「臭味相投」呢！你聽！孔子說了：「人之過也，各以其黨。觀過知人！」

勤勞和懶惰是人們的兩個好朋友。他們也找「臭味相投」的人而處。

如果那人散漫，浪蕩，不經心，不努力，只知享受，不願吃苦，只想乘涼，不願流汗，只求收穫，不願耕耘，懶惰便會跑去接近他，很自然地成為他的朋友，然後慢慢地帶他去接近貧乏、困頓、疾病、衰弱、痛苦、罪惡、失敗，甚至毀滅……。

如果那人踏實，肯幹，認真工作，不怕流汗，不怕吃苦，能耐勞，願盡心盡力，願動手動腳動腦，努力負責，勤勞便會喜歡他，接近他，送給他微笑，和他結為好朋友，帶給他富裕、健康、力量、快樂、滿足、榮譽和成功……。

相信你必然不喜歡貧乏、困頓、衰弱、痛苦、罪惡、失敗甚至毀滅，必然喜歡富裕、健康、力量、快樂、滿足、榮譽和成功！那麼，你要怎麼做，才能讓勤勞接近你，成為你的好朋友？

Hardworking

Things of a kind come together. This is the same from ancient. It's the rule created by the creator, is more the way the nurture of the universe, it can't be exchanged. Is it not so? Fire ignites the dry. Water flows to the wet. Is it not so? Cattle take grass. Cat takes fish. As to human being, isn't it the same? Ugly often gets gather toward evil man. Honor often belongs to kind man. Even do evil will friends attracted to each other by common tastes! Hear! Said by Confucius: "About the fault of person, belongs to party member. We can know a person in seeking his fault."

Hardworking and lazy are two good friends of the people. They will make the friends attracted to each other by common tastes.

If he is undisciplined, dissipated, careless, lack of hardworking, just want to live in easy and comfort, won't to bear hardship, just want to catch cool, won't to sweat streaming, seek harvest, won't to cultivated, lazy will go near him, make friends with him naturally, then brings him slowly to near poor, fatigued, disease, weak, agony, evil, fail, even extinguish…

If that person is dependable, willing to work, earnest, no afraid of sweat streaming, no afraid of bearing hardship, bear work, want to do as possible as he can, want to use his hands, feet and mind, hardworking and is responsible, hardworking will like and go near him, gift him smile, make friends with him, bring him well off, health, strength, happy, satisfied, honor and success…

I believe you are surely dislike poor, fatigued, disease, weak, agony, evil, fail, even extinguish, and like well off, health, strength, happy, satisfied, honor and success! Then, how will you do and let hardworking near you, make good friends with you?

用鋤頭寫詩

那個下午，我看見一名農夫在以鋤頭寫詩；造物則把詩寫在他身上。

在田園裡，他把鋤頭舉起來，鋤下去，然後又舉起來，鋤下去……。

他一鋤鋤地鋤下去。土鬆了，碎了，成溝了，成壟了……由點而線，由線而面……。

是了，這是一名農夫在用鋤頭寫詩了：一個字，一個詞，一個標點符號，相互結合、融貫，成為片語、詩行、詩節……。他要創造一首詩。

他要創造一首詩———一首田園詩。

更妙的是，沒想到造物則把詩寫在他身上！

看！他的肌肉，是那麼結實健壯，應該突顯出來的地方就突顯出來，應該低凹下去的地方就低凹下去，線條分明，協調勻稱；他的皮膚已成古銅色，正在陽光下閃閃發光。這本來就是一首詩了，再加上他不住地揮動著鋤頭，全身汗流如注，形成一幅動的畫面，更是一首詩———一首動的詩，力的詩！

他不住地把鋤頭舉起來，鋤下去，然後又舉起來，鋤下去……。

他一鋤一鋤地鋤下去……。

他是一名農夫。在田園裡，他用鋤頭寫詩；造物則把詩寫在他身上。

Write Poems with the Hoe

I found a farmer wrote poems with a hoe that afternoon; and the creator wrote poems on his body.

On the countryside, he raised the hoe, hoed down, raised the hoe once again, hoed down...

He hoes a hoe and another hoe. The soil is loosed, smashed, be in ditches, in ridges... from bits to lines, from lines to ranges...

Yes, it's a farmer in writing poems with the hoe: one word, one phrase, one punctuation mark, ties, blends, into idiom, phrase, line, stanza, section... He wants to create a poem.

He wants to create a poem-idyll.

The more wonderful thing is, it's not think of that the creator writes poems on his body.

Lo! His flesh is so stout so healthy and strong, projecting where it's ought to projecting, hollow where it's ought to hollow, clear in the line, curvy, well-balanced; his skin is bronzed, is shining under the sunshine. It's originally a poem, add to his wielding the hoe ceaselessly, sweat streaming on his body, forms a piece of tableau of alive, is more a poem - a poem of moving poem, a poem of force!

He raised the hoe, hoed down, raised the hoe once again, hoed down...

He hoed a hoe and another hoe...

He is a farmer. On the countryside, he writes poems with hoe, and the creator writes poems on his body.

新

　　新，翻新，更新。

　　新，日新，日日新，又日新。

　　日曆，撕去舊的一頁，出現新的一頁；撕去舊的一本，出現新的一本。——一天過了，又是新的一天；一年過了，又是新的一年。

　　房舍，住久了，或舊，或破漏，或不夠堅固舒適，翻新，換新。它的演化則由穴居而巢居，而草屋、木屋，而鋼筋水泥加上豪華裝潢有冷氣、空調的現代高樓大廈……。

　　除住，其他食衣行育樂諸民生活動不也如此？

　　長江後浪推前浪，一代新人換舊人。

　　新，新簇簇，煥然一新，光彩煥發。

　　新，充滿了希望，充滿了憧憬，充滿了未知，充滿了驚奇，充滿了夢想……。

　　新，有許多發展空間，成長空間，發展，發展，再發展，成長，成長，再成長……。

　　是名新生嬰兒，是一輪旭日，是一棵樹苗，紅冬冬的，光燦燦的，嫩綠綠的，好惹人憐，好惹人愛，好惹人讚賞不置！

　　新，進步的動力，好令人振奮，欲迎上前去！

　　新，翻新，更新。

　　新，日新，日日新，又日新。

　　新，最重要的是自新，自我觀念的創新。

New

New, renovation, renewal.

New, new a day, renew every of day, and new once a day.

Calendar, tears a leaf of old, appears a leaf of new; tears a copy of old , appears a copy of new. -a day is over, once more there is a new day; a year is over, once more there is a new year.

House, dwells for a long time, may old or broken, or no strong and comfortable enough, renovation, renewal. Its evolution is from live in caves to live in the nest, to live in house thatched with straw, wooden house, and to live in mansion made of steel bar and cement fitted with air condition...

Except dwelling, may it not the same of the livelihood about the others of food, dress, walk, education and entertainment?

In the Changjiang river the waves behind drive on those before, the new generation replaces the elder.

New, it's novelty, having a bright, new look, brilliance.

New full of hope, full of vision for future, full of unknown, full of surprise, full of dream...

New, it has great space of development, space of growth, development and development again, growth and growth again...

It's a new baby, a rising sun, a young plant, redden, brilliant, soft greenish, attracts pity, attracts love, how will be praised!

New, it's the power of progress, how will be bestir, want to head on!

New, it's renovation, renewal.

New, new a day, renew every of day, and new once a day.

New, the most important thing is start anew, bring forth original ideas of own concept.

希望

　　人是為了希望而活著的。人不能沒有希望；一旦沒有了希望，活著有什麼意義？倘若如此，生不如死。

　　希望是一座燈塔，指引航海者渡過茫茫大海，抵達彼岸。

　　希望是一盞明燈，引導著一個人走向光明的前程。

　　希望可能有好多。各人不一定每樣都擁有，或取其一，或取少許。一個人如有數個希望，總要有一個作為主要希望。那是他要盡最大力量，全力以赴的。

　　農人要耕地，以養天下之人。

　　工人要製器，以供利用。

　　商人要搬有運無，以便貨暢其流。

　　教師要教育好學生，使成有用。

　　軍人要保衛國家。

　　……

　　希望的達成如何？許是完全達成，許是部分達成，依能力、機遇而定。——當然每個人都希望以能力達成，不靠機遇。

　　努力達成希望，是人生一大樂事，所以人人希望達成希望，不致落入失望。

　　希望達成希望，只是希望，還是空的；最重要的是，努力以赴，達成希望。

Hope

Human being keeps alive in order to hope. Any person can't have hope; what is the meaning to keep alive without hope one day?

Hope is a light house, guides the sailor to sail across the vast ocean, to arrive the termination.

Hope is a bright lamp, guides a person to go on the bright future.

How nice the hope is. Uncertainly no everybody must hold it, may hold one, or some. If a person holds some hopes, he always will choice one to be his main hope. It's what he wants to put his most force to do with all his strength.

Farmer must to till the soil, for nurture all of the people.

Worker must to produce instruments for utilize.

Merchant must to convey materials for flowing.

Teacher must to teach students for them to be employed.

Soldier must to guard country.

…… ……

How to attain hope? May attain all, may attain some, decided by the ability, or opportunity. -of course, every one hope to attain owe to his ability, not to rely opportunity.

Make an effort to attain it is a joyful thing, so everyone hope to attain hope, not to loosed.

Wish to attain hope is a wish, it's still empty; the most important thing is made an effort to attain the hope.

年輕

我看到了年輕，悟出了年輕的意義。

在一座花園裡，種有各式各樣的花，朵朵盛開，萬紫千紅，芳香美麗。這就是年輕。年輕是盛開的花，萬紫千紅，芳香美麗。

在那炎炎夏日之中，烈陽曝曬著大地，盡情發揮它的熱力和光亮，令人們和大地上的萬物都有受不了的感覺。這就是年輕。年輕是發出無限熱力和光亮的夏日之午的烈陽。

那是一場運動會。參加徑賽的跑出最快的速度。參加跳高跳遠的跳出最高最遠的紀錄。參加鏢槍的擲出最遠的距離。參加球賽的盡最大的力量去比賽。……他們有如生龍活虎，付出了最大的努力，盡自己的所能，全心全力投入。這就是年輕。

那是一場盛大的閱兵典禮。受閱隊伍是那麼整齊，動作一致，一起提腿，一起跨步，腳步啪啪而響，雄赳赳，氣昂昂。這就是年輕。

那是哄堂大笑，是真誠的，坦率的，毫無掩飾，笑聲甚至帶有金屬相碰的鏗然。這就是年輕。

我看到了年輕，悟出了年輕的意義。

Young

I find out young, and make out the meaning of young.

There is a garden which planted every kind of flower, and bloomed of every one, they blaze of colour, fragrant and beauty. It is young. Young is the flower full blossom, blaze of colour, fragrance and beauty. It is young.

In the hot summer, scorching sun shine upon the earth, does its best to play the role of the hot force and bright, makes people and everything in the world holds the feeling unable to endure can't bear. It's young. Young is the scorching sun of summer play the role of the hot force and bright.

It's an athletic meeting. They make the fastest speed who takes part in track events. They make the highest and longest who takes part in high jump and broad jump. They make the longest distance who takes in javelin throw. They make the most force to match who takes part in ball game… They like a lively dragon and an active tiger, offer the most effort, put in their whole mind and effort. It's young.

It's a great dress parade. The reviewed troops are in so good order, action is in so unanimous, lift leg all together, stride all together, the steps sound in a clap after a clap, valiantly, high spirited. It's young.

It's all the people burst out, truly, frankly, not to conceal, even the sound of laugh carry jingle of the mental banged.

I find out young, and make out the meaning of young.

萬年長青

只要是萬年輕，是它的莖，是它的幹，隨便剪取一段，放進水裡，固定水中，它便活了，而且活得鮮綠，愉快，活得長青……

萬年輕，啊，萬年長青！

很快地，它的根便從被剪斷的地方長出，一絲絲，一縷縷，糾結纏繞，探向水中，去吸取養分，活得鮮綠，愉快，活得長青……

萬年輕，啊，萬年長青！

它不圖什麼享受，不擇什麼口味，絲毫不苛求，只要一缽水，乾淨也罷，骯髒也罷，它便能活得鮮綠，愉快，活得長青……

萬年輕，啊，萬年長青！

還要像什麼高貴的花木，要園丁去小心呵護，修剪，施肥，除草，驅蟲嗎？不需要！它早已活得鮮綠，愉快，活得長青……

萬年輕，啊，萬年長青！

挺著莖幹，撐著綠色劍葉，只要一缽水，一片陽光，它什麼都可以不要，什麼都可以不管，活得鮮綠，愉快，活得長青……

萬年輕，啊，萬年長青！

淡泊，自得，不作過分欲求，只有奉獻……

萬年輕，啊，萬年長青！

Flourish Forever

Just the rohdea japonica, may his stem, may his trunk, cut a section to place in the water, fixed in the water, he will live, and live into vernal, happy, and live into evergreen...

Rohdea japonica, oh, flourish forever!

In very soon, his root sprouts from the place where it's cut, a string and a string, a thread and a thread, tangle and twine, stretch toward the water, to inhale the nutrition, live to be vernal, happy, live to be evergreen...

Rohdea japonica, oh, flourish forever!

He conspires no of whatsoever enjoyment, selects no of whatsoever taste, be no too exacting, only one pot of water, pure can be, dirty can be, he can live into vernal, happy, and live into evergreen...

Rohdea japonica, oh, flourish forever!

May like the noble garden plants, need the gardener to preserve carefully, to clip, to fertilize, to weeding, to drive the worm? It's no need! He lives formerly into vernal, happy, and lives into evergreen...

Rohdea japonica, oh, flourish forever!

Straightens up the stem and trunk, holds the sword-like green leaf, just a pot of water, a piece of sunshine, he can't want whatsoever of anything, he can't matter whatsoever of anything, live into vernal, happy, and live into evergreen...

Rohdea japonica, oh, flourish forever!

Elegant and quiet, self-satisfied, no do more lust, just to offer as tribute...

Rohdea japonica, oh, flourish forever!

國家圖書館出版品預行編目

水琴 = The water lyre / 許其正著. -- 臺北市：
致出版, 2022.11
　　面；　公分
　　中英對照
　　ISBN 978-986-5573-46-1(平裝)

863.51　　　　　　　　　　111016486

水琴
The water lyre

作　　者／許其正
出版策劃／致出版
製作銷售／秀威資訊科技股份有限公司
　　　　　114 台北市內湖區瑞光路76巷69號2樓
　　　　　電話：+886-2-2796-3638
　　　　　傳真：+886-2-2796-1377
網路訂購／秀威書店：https://store.showwe.tw
　　　　　博客來網路書店：https://www.books.com.tw
　　　　　三民網路書店：https://www.m.sanmin.com.tw
　　　　　讀冊生活：https://www.taaze.tw

出版日期／2022年11月　　定價／300元

致　出　版　　　　　　　向出版者致敬